PHARMACY COLLEGE:
CRAZY *DAZE* AND HAZY NITES

Acknowledgments

*I wish to thank all those in my professional and
personal lives who made this book possible.*

Mr. Nick Productions, LLC

© 2017 by Mr. Nick Productions, LLC

Edited by my longtime friend and editor/writer,
Marilyn Milow Francis – Thank you!

Front and back covers – Jake Centofranchi
Book Layout – Jake Centofranchi

Photo of hapless pharmacy college graduate – Anonymous
Published by Mr. Nick Productions, LLC © 2017

ISBN : 978-0-692-85504-1

Dedications

To my wife, affectionately called *hottie blondie*, who lived through most of my crazy days and hazy nights as they were unfolding. And to my children, who may get a chuckle out of these stories.

Foreword

Those five years (six years, now) in pharmacy college weren't wasted, were they? They were the best five years of my life, right? It's hard to tell; it could have gone either way!

Although based on actual events, this is a book of humor and should be taken as such. There is no malicious intent; the only intent is to entertain!

Dr. I. Mayputz

TABLE OF CONTENTS

FIRST YEAR

FOURTH YEAR

FIFTH YEAR

Introduction

This book is about a slightly fictionalized account of
my life in pharmacy college, inspired by actual events.
Embellishments of strange happenings were unnecessary
because human foibles ran rampant. However, all names
and places have been changed so as not to embarrass the
guilty, inept and downright scurvy. The stories are retold
in a series of vignettes which best captured my mood at
the time. Science, pharmacy, medicine, and professionalism
were crammed daily into our skulls while many friends at
other colleges were being spoon-fed dubious liberal bullshit.
Those often bewildering and crazy college *daze* were
difficult and unrelenting. The hazy nites, however, were
often a welcome respite for the wickedly inclined. But if
you persevered, had a sense of humor, *inhaled* and imbibed
regularly, you would someday be a pharmacist. Was all the

stress and aggravation worth it? Was getting a high-paying job right out of college worth it? Was getting HIGH worth it? I think so, but I'm not completely sure. Nevertheless, I would definitely have done it all over again, even if just to meet that special *hottie blondie*, my future wife!

Enjoy.

Dr. I. Mayputz

FIRST YEAR

1

A "Real" Career

It was the late '70s, the Vietnam War was over, and I was a relatively content juvenile who fancied himself a naturalist/athlete. My adolescent spare time was largely devoted to bugs and sports. Either playing something athletically or chasing something with wings was my life in those post-pubescent years in my small, bucolic town in upstate New York. Not much happened there so you had to find things to do yourself. I embraced entomology at an early age but also had a penchant for competitive tennis and track. My father was a formidable tennis player and coach of the local college tennis team as well as being a professor of engineering at said college. So there I was, either on a tennis court banging forehands or in a field chasing down butterflies with my trusty net. Or, knee-deep in a local brook, looking for and finding salamanders. Such was my life during those long ago summers. School, however always seemed to get in the way of my passions. But I was an excellent student and seemed to excel in the sciences. I excelled in the humor department as well. O.K., I was the

3

class clown, but as I got older the core passions of my youth never faded. Sure, I dabbled in high-brow endeavors such as piano, plays, musicals, operettas and other high school extra-curricular *vices*. I even produced and acted in some original low-brow comedies with a bunch of like-minded sorts. It was fun and satisfying at the time. Nevertheless, the underlying current of my being still sought solace in all things creepy crawly. I just couldn't shake those bugs and slugs! The next fall I was starting my senior year in high school with nary a logical thought about my future. Medicine and science were the top contenders but nothing specific. Although my parents were both intelligent college professors, their guidance was next to nil. My father wrongly assumed that I would outgrow my "infantile" entomological leanings and become a stoic and dowdy civil engineer, like him. No frills, no thrills, no fun, but a job for "real" men. Enough of this foolishness with insects and mudpuppies. My mother, although a major influence on my youthful naturalistic pastime, was mute when it came to college and career decisions. It was assumed and implied that I would do the right thing and suddenly choose engineering as a vocation. Just like that. Needless to say, my current junior year was overloaded with very stressful undercurrents in my household. My gruff father had given me zero advice, zero talks and zero life plans. I was supposed to magically wake up one day and be an engineer and make everyone happy and proud. No pressure there!

For some unknown reasons, neither parent ever bothered
to have a serious conversation with me about ANYTHING
scholastic as I approached the zenith of my high school tenure.
Whenever I mentioned the possibility of medical school or
any science-type endeavor, I was immediately shot down.
"What if you finish undergrad with a B average in Biology,
then what will you do?" my father would always say. "YOU
can't get into medical school with a B average. What would
be your plan B? And what undergrad college would you go
to, anyway? We're not connected and you're not brilliant."
And that was that. I was a loser from the get go. No one was
helping me so why even try? I might as well have applied to
Clarkson University, become an engineer, and got it over with.
That was my destiny, or was it? I would be working in a small
nearby pharmaceutical plant as a bottle washer during the
upcoming summer vacation and thought that perhaps a job
in a science field would be *cool*. But what exactly would that
futuristic job be? I was confused and conflicted. I consulted
many high school friends; they were useless. I had no real
girlfriend to talk to either. I did have a best friend, however,
he was determined to apply to pharmacy college. Hmm…
pharmacy college? Science/biology/chemistry equals a job
right out of college? Maybe I should consider that? There was a
college night coming up at my parent's college with a pharmacy
college in attendance. I was going to go and see what happens.
At least I could get a brochure.

2

College Night

I didn't go by myself, perhaps I should have. My old man went with me. It was held in the large gymnasium at his place of employment. He was an engineering professor and knew many of the visiting college reps. He steered me away from the "obvious" pricey colleges, the "LIBERAL" Ivy League colleges, and rolled his eyes and sighed deeply whenever I expressed even the faintest interest in a particular university. My father thought all of this was a gigantic waste of time. He knew better. Until, of course, we chanced upon the engineering college tables. Clarkson, RPI, and RIT (Pop's alma mater) were some of the culprits present. My father personally knew those guys and instantly started chitchatting with them. Like-minded and self-important, those were the blokes to listen to. Unfortunately, while he was busy adulating the choir, I snuck off to the pharmacy college table to see what they were peddling, and gleaned from the reps as much as I could before my dad brusquely showed up. He was not pleased at my disappearance and admonished me for being so rude in front of his buddies. After all, I was going to be an engineer. I tucked the pharmacy college brochure into my coat and we went home. Nothing was said, as usual. After all, I was going to be an engineer!

3

The Phone Call

I had really enjoyed my summer job at the nearby pharmaceutical plant before my senior year. I was employed as the head bottle washer and cleaner of dirty beakers, glassware, etc. It was a busy place but I never broke a single piece of equipment. So what, it was a job. I was grateful for the extra money and experience working with real scientists. I still had enough time during the evenings and weekends to play tennis and catch my fill of butterflies and other critters. Senior year had started and we had to meet with our guidance counselors that September to get our lives figured out. Mr. T. was a former shop and agriculture teacher who was promoted to guidance counselor. We had met many times since ninth grade for course selection and future plans. So there we were, in his tiny orifice next to the nurse's station, staring at each other, not knowing what to say. The room was full of brochures from local two-year and community colleges– that's where the majority of our "farming community" high-schoolers ended up going.

8

You know, to learn about John Deere tractors, animal
husbandry, artificial insemination of cattle, herding, treating
rashes on cow teats, etc. Useful stuff if you were going to
inherit daddy's farm. Dismissively I looked blandly at those
brochures. "What do you want to do, Izzy?" he asked,
also rather blandly. "Something in biology." I answered.
He knew my grades were top notch, especially in all the
science classes. But curiously he never mentioned any Ivy
League colleges. Perhaps I wasn't that smart after all. And
he knew I wasn't connected in any way. Legacy? What
was that? Anyway, we spoke for a while; the subject of
engineering came and went. No interest whatsoever. Finally
I blurted out near the end of our session that maybe I just
might be interested in pharmacy. I still had that pharmacy
brochure from last year's college night carefully tucked
away in my top dresser drawer in my bedroom. I admit
to whipping it out occasionally and musing about being a
pharmacist, whatever that was. I mean I had been inside
drugstores many times but never really knew exactly what
a druggist did besides selling pills. Mr. T. nearly jumped
out of his shoe tops when I mentioned the word pharmacy.
He told me to stay right where I was; he'd be right back.
He quickly vanished into his adjacent inner office and
proceeded to phone someone. I could barely make out some
muffled laughter, and there was lots of silence. What was
he doing in there, on my time? But he had told me to stay.

What was up? He returned just as abruptly and proceeded
to shake my hand vigorously up and down, as if he was
milking it. His Cheshire cat grin never left him as he
loudly congratulated me for getting into pharmacy college.
What??!! No grades were sent, no SAT scores reported, no
teacher recommendations obtained. What??!! Evidently the
two-hour away pharmacy college had a predilection for
accepting qualified small-town boys and girls. All he had to
do was contact the dean of admissions and plead my case.
And that's exactly what he did, and I got in, over the phone!
The rest of the required documentation and materials would
be formally sent later. His word was good enough for the
dean and I was all set. Really I was dumbstruck. He patted
me on the back as I left his office, still smiling about a job
well done, on his part. I told some of my pals; they were
in disbelief. I told my best friend who was going to apply
to the same college later in the fall like normal students
did; he was pissed off at me. I had stolen his thunder, and
maybe his spot in pharmacy college as well. But it wasn't
on purpose. I had just gone in there as required to get
some ideas together for college applications and walked out
practically a pharmacist. I told my parents at dinnertime
that evening. My father just stared at me without speaking.
As a professor, he knew the application process, etc. This just
couldn't be, or could it? My mother remarked that I would
make good money and there were plenty of jobs available, or

so she heard. My father lightened up and quickly acquiesced to the idea of me being a pharmacist. Now this was a clever plan. Even if I ended up with a B average, I would still be a pharmacist. There was no need for a plan B. This was going to be it. And it was full of SCIENCE, which I professed to love. This could be better than engineering. Blasphemous but brilliant! Of course I still had to go to college and all, and it would be no picnic, as I soon began to realize. And it was a five year program…

4

The Drive-by

I had just gotten into college; it was time for a fall road trip
to check it out. That's what you did back in the late '70s.
You got into your trusty station wagon and hit the road. My
father knew exactly where the pharmacy college was located.
He had made numerous trips to that town for professorial
conferences and had passed it on many occasions. It is
funny how he never told me about those trips; I had never
asked, I guess. Of course, I had never expressed an interest
in pharmacy before… Anyhow, I assumed we would spend
some time in the town, look at the college, step inside, maybe
even hobnob with some pharmacy students. It was going to
be exciting! My sister and mother were also going. The whole
damn family piled into our 1965 F-85 Oldsmobile station
wagon. I had heard that the pharmacy college was small
but part of a larger university which was located in a nearby
city. I was all atwitter as I closed the car door. My pop said
nothing. I also knew it had no dorms– that turned out to be
a problem in the very near future. But today, it was time for

a quickie two-hour trip, just to get the feel of the drive and
to show me the school. It was fun trekking through winding
mountainous back roads from our puny village; over hills and
dales, through gullies and gulches. Small talk consumed us
during the trip. Two hours later the town appeared. OK, what
do we do first? Pop drove straight through downtown as if
on a Messianic mission, aiming right for the college. No time
for eating, drinking, defecating, or sightseeing. No worries;
soon the university grounds would appear and we could
officially park on "MY" campus. There would be food, water
and bathrooms. I eagerly fondled that well-worn pharmacy
brochure I still had from college night and anticipated
buildings and green spaces galore. I grew up in a small college
town, where my parents were professors, so I kind of knew
what a bustling college was supposed to look and "feel" like.
We were driving slowly on that Saturday when suddenly
my father abruptly pointed to his right. We all swiveled
our heads in unison to look. There it was: a red brick, ivy-
covered lone building resembling a very tiny high school. We
drove by, stared and kept going. Good thing I didn't blink.
Are you kidding me? That was it? How disappointing. Of
course the brochure did not show any "distance" shots, only
closeups of the college. I had been duped. Dad turned the car
around and headed back toward it, intending to find some
parking area. He pulled into the 10-slot college parking lot
and stopped the car. There were nine other parking spots

available. It was quiet, too quiet. I naïvely bounded for the front door but stopped briefly to read the small, nondescript sign on the teeny-weeny front lawn; it resembled one of those campaign signs you stick in the grass. It read, "PP College of Pharmacy." I bolted up the marble steps and found a locked front door and an aged bronze sign that read Closed on Saturday, Sunday. Open Weekdays from 8 a.m. to 5 p.m. There were no students, no professors, no life. I swear I heard distant laughter coming from nearby motorists as I futilely tugged at that big brass front door, looking like Dorothy being rebuffed at the entrance to the Emerald City in the *Wizard of Oz*. I was embarrassed. I went back to the car and we headed quickly to the nearest Mobil gas station (that's the brand my father used) for a bathroom break and a Snickers bar apiece. I think we shared a 7-Up that day, also. My father then asked me rather enthusiastically if I liked the school. What? What could I say? He was going to pay for it and I was already committed to going. I kind of nodded half-heartedly as we began our trip back home. It was NOT what I had envisioned at all! This was going to be my bleak confinement for five years. Could I take it? I wasn't sure. To my father, it was a place of learning. Beauty and comfort had nothing to do with anything educational in his book. He smiled, I pouted. Our ride home was quiet but I did manage to throw out that damn pharmacy college brochure, out the passenger side window. I littered, so fine me!

5

Pharmacy Buds

My best friend also received a positive nod and got into pharmacy college, in the spring of our senior year, when you were supposed to. He was relieved. It was a minor miracle since the college usually picked only one candidate per small town/village; that was their MO, in hopes of the graduates returning to said home towns to set up shop. That way, New York State would always have an evenly spread bevy of pharmacists, from corner to corner. Of course, those were the olden days, with privately owned drugstores. The chain-pharmacies were just starting their insidious encroachments; their explosion in the years hence changed the archaic and parochial approach to pharmacy manpower (and it was mostly men in those days, too). Anyway, two best buds would be enrolled in pharmacy college together; how cool was that? But seriously, as the summer dwindled down, my housing situation was just not materializing. Many anguishing phone calls to the college's housing office produced leads but no leases. Perhaps I was asking for too much. I didn't realize that because the college had no dorms, I had to find private housing myself. The college DID have a *greasy* cafeteria that closed at 2 p.m. Hell, the entire school closed at 5 p.m.! My parents, although both college professors, always seemed put out and feigned ignorance at my dire plight. I desperately needed assistance and they did the ostrich thing. I'm not sure why. It's as if they didn't quite believe I was actually leaving. Whatever, I needed help. We should have gotten into the station wagon, driven the two hours, stayed overnight and really beat the pavement until I found a place to live. No such luck. I had also forgotten that my parents were extremely allergic to hotels, motels and restaurants. I was a young driver and didn't have a car, didn't know the way, and didn't have a checkbook, etc. Otherwise, I would have gone myself. I was doomed. I called my best friend and HE helped me, thank goodness. He had found lodging in a small house, on a quiet street and about a 20-minute walk from the school. He recommended me to the landlord, who would be living there as well, and he acquiesced. The extra income was also appreciated by him. The landlord cleaned out an outsized closet, fumigated it, and it became my new bedroom. I was just grateful and thankful. The landlord also promised to cook dinners and feed us if we bought the food. This was sounding better and better. Although I hadn't seen the place or met the leaseholder, my friend assured me things were

on the square and I would be okay with it. I trusted him.
So, there would be two of us, plus the landlord and his dog.
My parents were cluelessly elated. I was all set. Although my
friend did say that the landlord was the cantor and senior
music director at a major Catholic church in town, and a
bit strange. What? Strange in what way? We would both
find out as time unfolded, but for now I had a place to live.
I was thinking of what rock-and-roll records to bring; this
college gig was going to be alright!

6

Kaiser

He would have put a police dog to shame; wait a minute, perhaps he was one? Our first meeting was downright scary. I was moving into my first home-away-from-home with the new landlord present, as well as my parents. Even my sister chipped in to help her big brother move in. All of a sudden, a big flash of "barking blackness" darted out from behind the house at full speed and made a beeline for us helpless humans on the front lawn. At the top of his lungs and, in a rich baritone voice mind you, the landlord/church cantor yelled, "Kaiser, STOP!" Dutifully, the dog hit the brakes and immediately obeyed. Growling, tongue hanging out, panting, eyes darting between us, head cocked to one side; he looked comical trying to understand the situation. We were on his turf and needed to be attacked and mauled, and here his master made him sit like a puppy. How disgraceful. But maybe these strangers were friends? He squirmed uncomfortably as each of us in turn petted, hugged, and spoke to him. The bonding was brief but profound. Within minutes he was wagging his long tail and walking amongst us as if we were all his dear old pals. What a dog, what a smarty-pants! This large, black German shepherd turned out to be a trusted companion, an excellent guard dog, and loyal friend. I still miss him.

7

The Freshman Orientation Picnic

It was nothing special. A college/fraternity sponsored
and organized kegger a few days before classes started for
incoming freshmen at a large park near the school. Well, not
that near. We freshmen had to find rides to get there, and
we all did. No one missed it. It was deemed that important.
And, lots of upperclass frat brothers showed up to run the
party and scope out the freshmen chicks. It was a party,
that's all. Or was it? People talking, playing Frisbee, drinking
beer, laughing and bonding. That is correct: bonding. There
were approximately 114 fresh-faced would-be pharmacists
(50/50 male and female) and, maybe 30 medical technology
students (all female) at that get-together. And it seemed that
within a short amount of time we all knew each other; kind
of like at a military boot camp. We were *special* and felt an
instant kinship. It was a good, perhaps elitist, feeling. We
were pharmacy students, not plain old liberal arts dunces in
a typical university. These would be my brothers and sisters
for the difficult five-year duration. Most of the students came

from disparate parts of the state, mostly from insignificant small towns and villages. No city slickers here. It was an intentional design by the college. In those days, most small towns boasted a locally owned drugstore. The thinking was that pharmacy graduates would return home, buy out the "old" druggists and continue servicing the local populations. Of course the chain drugstores changed that kind of small-minded thinking in a hurry. Anyhow, I vividly remember most of the teen-aged men and women in my freshman class as being above average in looks and mind, even from that brief party interaction. Most of us came from the same socioeconomic strata of life, dressed about the same, acted and spoke about the same. I'm generalizing, of course. However, it was comforting to feel comfortable with strangers you just met. It was unlike the students I met in dental school years later, most of whom looked as though they came from the island of misfit toys! Anyway, we ended up losing about one third of our pharmacy college classmates before third year started. But the remaining hard-boiled bunch of us, both male and female, stuck together psychologically. And physically, as well. Intra-school dating was wide-spread and popular. The running joke was that our small college functioned as a free dating service. Outsiders, such as transfer students, were usually not welcome into our already tightly knit social structures. That's how profoundly that first party had touched us. Well, at least I was touched; maybe in the head.

8

English Rules!

Could have fooled me, at least as a relatively naïve
freshman pharmacy student. But then again, everything
was new to me as a beginner. This was pharmacy college
and yet my first year schedule was composed of Biology
(Botany/Zoology), English (Speech/Writing), Calculus
I and II, Inorganic Chemistry I and II, and Intro. to
Pharmacy. Yay, there it was– a pharmacy course, at last.
The set list of classes were necessary evils to hurdle over
before the main courses started in succeeding years. You
just had to be patient and perseverant. I mean, how hard
could these "pre" courses be? Plenty, and let me tell you,
not the ones you thought would be, either. Botany/Zoology
was taught, and I use that word facetiously in this instant,
by a long tenured, very likable but disorganized and flaky
entomologist. The lectures were a joke, the labs somewhat
worthwhile, and tests– unpassable. Without old exams
to study and memorize from, we all would have received
F's. Calculus was fair, straightforward and lectured by a

handsome, newly hired basketball wizard/engineer out of U...n College who also doubled as our school's basketball coach. He ended up his 40-plus year career as the provost of the college. Not bad for starting out as a lowly calculus and economics professor, bouncing a ball. Inorganic Chemistry was over my head. The pipe-smoking and smug-looking prof used to teach at RPI to "real" science nerds and was a brainiac himself. I struggled, studied and struggled some more. It was frustrating to think that there would be so much more chemistry to come in future courses and here I was exhibiting such mediocrity in the opening salvo called freshman chem! How disheartening and disappointing.
I made it though, with the curve, of course. Intro to Pharmacy was a waste of time. English, English, English... This is where the rubber hit the road. Coming out of high school, I was regarded as a decent speaker, communicator and expresser of ideas on paper. I was praised by many teachers and students alike for my thought provoking compositions and especially my writing. However, as a freshman pharmacy peon, it didn't take a young and peevish looking Dr. D. long to call out my speaking and writing styles as pieces of shit, with appropriate grades reflecting my so-called abilities. WTF? Didn't she realize I was supposed to be a good writer? Didn't she get the memo? Apparently not. Most of my buddies also suffocated under this tyrannical witch that sought to break us down and

teach only HER way of public oration and writing. I would
have put up with her self-righteous treachery had the course
been easy. But no, she made it the most arduous class of
the first year. I studied harder and wasted more hours in
speech rehearsals and writing endeavors than I did for all
the other courses combined. I was going to be a pharmacist
dammit, not an English major! Give me a break. Now, did
most of us freshmen fools simultaneously laugh and cringe
as we took turns speechifying at that damn lectern? You bet.
And did most (including myself) students learn anything
useful from those difficult and dogmatic classes? Probably.
But here is the ironic part: I received a low B average from
her, and sure, the wasted time on English cost me in the
other classes, but the upshot of this was my wholehearted
abandonment of all her "principles" after completion of her
courses. I can honestly say that I learned all my composition
and writing skills from my eighth grade grammar instructor
and my high school creative writing teacher. That English
professor only gave high marks to like-minded souls. If
you became HER clone, a suck-up and brown nose, and
wrote in HER style, you got an A. The rest of us shitheads
just suffered. In my *humble* opinion, this pompous prof
squelched the oratory and writing talents of many students
and made "English" a miserable experience and hard to
get an A in. Well, I didn't give up on myself after being
ridiculed and belittled by her, and here I am, still putting

pen to paper, and receiving compliments and monies for my labors and *writing style!* And my gamut of publications has ranged from peer reviewed scientific and naturalistic literature to comedic fare, as well. I hope I run into her someday; on second thought, for her sake, I hope I don't.

9

Big H Sauce

Was I addicted or what? I was away from home for a short time and already had tasted, chewed and swallowed many foods that were "foreign" to me, such as broccoli, asparagus, steak prepared rare instead of like shoe leather, and, Big H Sauce. My Mom was a great cook but some foods had been omitted from our household and others could have been prepared differently. Big H Sauce, a Hellmann's product, was basically similar to Thousand Island Salad Dressing and McDonald's "special sauce," found in the Big Mac burgers. Well, I ended up slathering it on everything in sight. Bread, meats, salads, you name it. Even foody care packages from home got a tasty condiment poured over them by me. My high school best friend F., whom I roomed with at the time, became concerned at my usage of said product. We had an agreement with our landlord that he would cook dinner for us if F. and I chipped in monies for the food. I bought the "sauce" with my own meager allowance and would whip it out at dinnertime, much to the chagrin and astonishment of the landlord. He prided himself in his culinary imagination and skills and felt insulted by the inappropriate open jar standing there at supper. I finally "got the message" and by the end of October my consumption of that delicious topping had ceased. In retrospect, what had actually happened to me? Why did I become so gaga over a damn dressing anyway? Perhaps my taste buds were so deprived after years of neglect and needed to wake up? After seventeen years on the lam from bland cooking, they returned, or perhaps I had an addictive personality and needed to be careful for fear of this happening again. Next time it could be something more sinister and serious. I did some soul searching and, of course, blamed my Mom. Hellmann's eventually stopped making that darn tasty sauce. It was fun while it lasted, and I still remember it and miss it.

10

Roscoe's

It was autumn in the late '70s and I was 17 years old
and a freshman in pharmacy college. And I had a beer
in my hand thanks to Roscoe's, the "pharmacy bar" near
the downtown area. How did this come to pass? Well, the
cellar-dwelling student union at our college was dinky,
antiquated and a joke. Plus, it closed at 5 p.m., along with
the rest of our college. Roscoe's became our surrogate
nighttime place of sin, revelry and alcohol. Oh, it was legit
alright. Pharmacy banners dating back decades lined the
walls. All pharmacy students, past and present, were always
welcome. The drinking age back then was 18; nevertheless,
if you had a college I.D., you would gain instant entrance.
Hence the beer in my hand at age 17! All the bartenders
were pharmacy students. It was a hole in the wall, cheesy,
always crowded, with cheap vinyl covered furnishings in
the four, cramped booths. However, we didn't care. It was
an extension of our woeful college. What better place to
go to commiserate, TRY to pick up chicks, play foosball,

have a few drinks, and feel like you belonged somewhere. This mostly stand-up bar held a special place in all our hearts and minds throughout my tenure at PP College of Pharmacy. It was a drinking and dating emporium, and we all knew it, even the women! Riley, the bouncer and greeter, knew everyone and we all payed homage to him as if he was part of the pharmacy family. He was a good guy, he let everyone in. There were no fights, and there were rarely any townies present, except during the summers when we all went home. Locals knew to stay away because WE "owned the joint." The owner was happy with the steady influx of newbie frosh initiates that would become regulars in no time flat. But during our freshman year, a minor schism occurred. Uh oh! Three buildings down from there was a very modern, roomy pub called Mama's. Across the street there was Groucho's Bar and a few blocks away was the Legg Room. Somehow, Mama's had enticed us that fall, for whatever reason, and we abandoned Roscoe's en masse and migrated there because of their twelve for a dollar steamed clam specials and better foosball table. This went on intermittently all fall with the scuttlebutt in school being that we were the first freshmen class to screw Roscoe's. Well, it didn't last. A few fights with local assholes, a few bad clams, and we were back in the fold of our mother bar: Roscoe's. All was well in our limited universe, again. I remember the dented old juke box in the corner. Same songs every night: *Brown Eyed Girl, Cocaine, Mack the Knife.* Same old artists: Van Morrison, Journey, Bob Seeger, George Thorogood and Eric Clapton. I started to hate the repetition but I never put any money in that music machine. I was too busy playing foosball and getting good at the game. Others played Space Invaders, and later Pac Man video games. Many couples formed due to Roscoe's, or at least it facilitated the dating game. After I "officially" met my future wife at a private party up the street, we, of course, walked to Roscoe's as a normal couple looking to keep on talking and drinking. Roscoe's was magical and a welcome respite from the drudgery and stress of pharmacy college. Now, the administration knew for years where to find many of us miscreants in the evenings on most nights. But, to be honest, most of our school's real dweebs never frequented the place; it was their loss. Only the "cool" kids beat a path to Roscoe's, year after year, night after night. My father-in-law (class of '61) had been a bartender there and met/served my mother-in-law (nursing student) at the bar. Anyhow, things changed. Long after we graduated with fond memories, the drinking age leapt upward, Riley left, the owner sold out, new pharmacy students suddenly became serious folk, the college built a real student union, etc. I heard the pharmacy banners came down, the ceiling tiles with our names on it were white washed and the new owner was in business for money. Period. End of the line. But it was a good run. Many happy memories, many happy evenings spent playing foosball; many happy nights shooting the shit there with my many girlfriends. Roscoe's is still there, but it is no longer the bastion and sanctuary of pharmacy camaraderie. It is now merely a cold building serving cold beer and alcohol, with a small, unisex bathroom in the back. Nostalgia can be a cold bitch.

11

Meeting Mary Jane

You could have easily called me unworldly, a goody-two-shoes, or blamed my fellow hokey hucksters in high school. Whichever, or all three! I had never smoked dope before; never even smelled it. As a teenager I had never done anything illicit in the "drug world." Taking an aspirin for a headache or Kaopectate for diarrhea was about it. Ironically I was now ensconced in a legit drug world: pharmacy college. Of course I had learned about pot as a high-schooler in health class and had known many students that "smoked." The well-known *party* college in my hometown was the source of all the reefer that trickled over to the high school. Anyhow, I never saw it, never touched it, or even had any interest in it. Contrary to popular TV shows and media at the time, there was no usual "bad element" in my high school just itching to get us dweebs hooked on weed. So, there I was, a so-called mature and smart freshman at pharmacy college, eager and most willing to try some new things, expand my horizons, so to speak. It was late

September of my first year and I was restless. So I ventured
forward. Nevertheless, after only a few get-togethers at
private apartments (we had no dorms back then), it quickly
dawned on me that certain revelers smoked dope and
others did not. There was a strict delineation going on; two
distinct groups of partiers. I was in neither bunch, at least
at the beginning. I was new, what the hell? The "smokers"
all seemed to know each other and held court in secluded
circles during the parties. I was usually handed a free beer
at the door and left alone to partake in the party. Mingling
with other freshmen was the norm, but I wanted more.
Was it simple curiosity? I didn't know if I wanted to toke
or not but I was damn intrigued. I just had to try it, but
how? Mind you, one drug offense at our pharmacy college
meant expulsion. And yet students managed to "light
up" regularly and "smoke" as normal college students did
around the country. I'm sure our administration wussies
knew everything that we cretins were indulging in but what
were they to do; raid party after party and expel more than
half the student body? I think not. So, nothing happened.
Anyway, at one of those classic pharmacy college parties
I finally had my chance. I boldly entered the smoke-filled
kitchen area and matter-of-factly sat down in an empty
chair at the table. No one said a word, just some nods from
upperclassmen. A senior smiled and passed me the large
white stick going around, like a baton at a track relay. I

gingerly grasped it, took a tentative hit, handed it to the giggly girl on my right, and promptly left the group. I didn't belong there and I knew it. It seemed forced and unsanitary. But that's how we shared the doobs in those days; lips to lips. We didn't worry about personal cross contamination. Hepatitis A, herpes, HIV, and infected saliva didn't concern us. That's the kind of shit patients got; we were bullet-proof students! I had a few more beers in the living room, bantered small talk with some friends, and nervously waited for the ganja to take effect. Nothing unusual happened. Maybe I didn't inhale deeply enough; perhaps I didn't do something right? Disappointed, I trundled on home to my apartment. Maybe this whole weed thing was overblown hyperbole? Perhaps it didn't work on me? Perhaps.

12

Action Central

Part frat house, part "Greek" house, all action, all of
the time. At least that's what fellow students were led to
believe by we freshmen foursome. It started with a move
that fall by my landlord from an unassuming small house
in another part of town to a very large, three floor, gray-
colored, Victorian mini mansion, complete with a fire
escape ladder on the side and a finished attic. And he also
took his faithful dog, Kaiser, and my best friend F. with us.
The rent was the same but the walk to school was farther.
The neighborhood was okay, no overt crime that we could
see in the daytime, and a movie theatre, grocery store, and
pharmacy nearby. A sensible upgrade. However, the landlord
informed us that he needed more renters in a hurry to
meet his increased mortgage demands. No problem, he had
the rooms available and WE put the word out, instantly.
Sure enough, we got a bite right away. It turns out P. was
disgruntled with his present living conditions and said yes
to our spacious and inviting offer. Plus, we already knew

him as that *smart* and serious kid who also liked to party.
Now we needed one more sucker. Another bad housing/
roommate situation caused J. to materialize out of nowhere
and after a strenuous initiation– we three, plus the landlord,
dressed up in suits just to spoof him– he was unanimously
selected to join Action Central, an address and destination
coined by our strange landlord. The name stuck; in our
minds, and later, in the minds of our classmates. Four
straight guys from the same class, a straight dog and a
landlord of dubious sexual orientation! We all suspected
him of having an alternate lifestyle but it was never proven.
But his own dog would never sleep with him in his attic
chambers. Very interesting. Anyhow, now we could really let
loose, maybe. The landlord had his house rules, etc. and he
did cook dinner for us nightly if we chipped in the money
and bought the food. It was a fair deal at the beginning
but became cumbersome when partying, fraternization and
late night romps got in the way. He took it all in stride and
never admonished anyone, although, he was fond of saying
some profound and dispiriting axioms, directed at our
alleged debauchery. But he was a fun guy. We had a stamp
made that read Action Central, stamped our books with
it, and pretended that we were part of something special.
That October we started seriously planning for our first
party, doing so besides watching Reggie Jackson and the
suddenly relevant Yanks in the World Series. It would be

held before finals and be a small affair, so we thought. But we were ready; no fellow students yet knew of our existence but we were determined to change that. One small problem was our last roommate, whom we started calling Johnson. Although happy to be a part of something, he nevertheless shied away from the actual details of having rancorous and illicit fun. None of us planned to join a legal school fraternity because we now had our own. And yet he still seemed to pine for legitimacy and made fruitless forays to join a college frat. He never went through with it, however, and settled in with us deviants for the year. We planned to have fun, fun, fun and maybe even get some girls in on the action, if you know what I mean. That's how we thought back then. Action Central was up and running. Where were all the girls at? WE WERE READY. My new, fellow-freshman girlfriend (aka Tumbleweed) at the time didn't approve of our seedy "plans," but what could she do? None of my house pals had a steady partner except for "lucky" me. However, we were all in this together, but more like the Four Stooges than the Four Muskateers! We were ready; really? We were all of 18 years old, apiece!

13

A Proper Stoning

After that disappointing initial inhalational foray into the realm of dope, this *dope* refrained from "smoking" and never gave it a second thought. My freshman girlfriend didn't do it; I followed suit. The freshmen courses were hard enough to cope with; I didn't want to be distracted with reefer madness, as well! Or so I sarcastically thought. Parties came and went; I went to most of them, but still, I didn't put lips to rolling paper. First semester was slowly and blessedly coming to an end and holiday time off was at hand. No more calculus, English, botany, inorganic chemistry, and pharmacy intro. courses to worry about. At least, not till second semester. But then two of my three roommates revealed to me that they had gotten "stoned" recently and loved it. How did that happen? I was envious because of my previous ineptitude. Why wasn't I invited? Where did it happen and when? I was mad as hell. Anyway, regardless of their conflicting stories, they definitely wanted to include me the next time they sparked a bowl or pinner. What? All this new lingo and slang to learn. I was really out of the loop and pissed off, particularly because I always prided myself on being *in the know!* Here my roommates went and had "fun" behind my back. They knew I would be steamed but did it anyway. However, I didn't have to wait long for the opportunity to *inhale.* We three roommates, minus Johnson, and with our landlord's permission, planned a small Friday night, BYOB party prior to the semester final exams at our huge boarding house which we affectionately called Action Central. Most of our friends and upperclassmen facetiously called it that name although there really wasn't much "action" going on at the time. Only I had a girlfriend. It was entirely hype, until that fateful party. It was December and it was snowing heavily outside. Maybe no one would show up. We had told many students about the party and were anxious about the turnout. Well, the front door bell starting ringing and ringing. Snow-covered guys and gals pushed past our growling German shepherd, threw off their wet coats, put the suds and wine down, and sat where there was room. Even my girlfriend showed up. The obvious nerds (formerly us) of our class were not there, obviously. Just the *cool* kids, you know. Rock music, laughter, beer, wine and Mary Jane. You can guess what happened. It was a rather reckless night of drinking and participating in all the *smoking* rituals of the day. Joints, bongs, pipes were at the ready and fully charged and functional. A red-eyed, slightly

paranoid Mayputz with the munchies and a rapid pulse
rate had a mind altering evening but went to bed solo. The
next morning (good thing it was Saturday) I remembered
all the profound and interesting conversations I had with
guests but couldn't actually think of specifics. My two close
roommates found me recovered but somewhat woozy at
breakfast. Johnson, that feckless fourth housemate, who
did NOT party with us, made a scene, nevertheless, and
disapproved of the direction we were taking Action Central
in. I remember thinking long and hard about the choices I
had made during that party and the tone of our household
relationships. During that historic party, the landlord had
briefly appeared, nodded to us and promptly vanished
upstairs. He didn't care, his dog didn't care; as long as we
paid the rent on time, all was kosher. But was I now going
to be called a stoner, a degenerate, and forever labeled as
one? And would that agnostic Johnson leave our house and
tattle on us? Was I still paranoid? All these new thoughts
were bubbling to the surface at once. We three decided to
downplay the whole recent event; meanwhile, in school, a
buzz picked up that the *boyz* at Action Central were not
only cool cats but hosts of fantastic parties (we had only
one thus far). Action Central was reborn that night. Now
we could play up the hype and perhaps start having some
other kind of action, from the feminine side of the species.
At least for my pals. Maybe? And Johnson? Well, he also

wisely decided to play it cool, not make waves and let us have our tainted fun, as he put it. Whatever. Although he was always welcome to *JOINT* us he never did. Sex, drugs and rock-and-roll slowly crept into Action Central and we three reveled in it. We were paltry "rock stars" in our dinky college but became popular, even as freshmen. But again it was sometimes difficult to separate fact from fiction. We studied hard, pretended to party hard, and kept up the hard-core mystique and personas. Even Johnson got some undeserved notoriety, that horseshitter. In hindsight, it was truly more fiction than fact. Nonetheless, the "stories" still circulated. The seeds of partying were sown at Action Central and would continue to grow deep into second year as well. As for me, my growing eccentric and eclectic personality started to gain traction, and more.

14

The Smallman Riseth

Steve Martin's late '70s, seminal comedy LP record *Let's Get Small* was inspirational to we freshmen. The particular title track (same name) was a clever spoof on getting high. After that popular album was issued, becoming "small" became another subcultural euphemism for getting stoned on pot. And gradually did rise the Smallman: me. This controversial and usually whispered nickname was given to me by my closest smokees during the first half of freshman year. I didn't object; you are what you are, or at least a close facsimile thereof! In my small college, most of the "hip" students eventually heard of the Smallman and also started referring to me by my reefer name; it became my moniker. Some peeps didn't even know my real name. Smallman became my nom deguerre. But was it all just hype and college gossip? Was it all just juicy school drama? My pals and I believed it was all in good fun; collegial experimentation, inhaling, exhaling and dealing. Dealing? Well, on a very minute level, mind you. Selling a gram here, a dime bag of "Columbian Gold" there; you know how it goes. But hardly worth the miniscule profit that was made. Alcohol was also on the college menu, but neither I or my friends became heavy drinkers. Sure, a dollar could buy four Bud (Budweiser) splits at local bars at the time, and sure, nearly everyone I knew had a brewsky regularly. But we didn't get stupid. We were just smart enough and sober enough to learn what we were paying tuition for. Lighting up a "j" or indulging in an after-dinner bong hit were our usual vices but not even on a daily basis. The manufactured school rumors, innuendos, and perceived bad boy images were mostly just that– half truths. By senior year things started to taper off. Part time jobs, love interests, maturity, etc. became weedkillers and effectively squelched our smoking horseplay. It had been a good run however, and I still have a few tokens saved from those halcyon toker *daze*. Pharmacy college had been very hard academically but I sometimes miss the hazy and smoky times. The Smallman retired years ago but the memories and hash pipe are still around.

15

The Foosball Wizard

I first met him at the freshman disorientation picnic.
He was very skinny, had glasses and a mop top of wispy,
brown curly hair. He seemed a bit brash and condescending
and we had only interacted for a short while. Was he just
another nervy and nerdy *nebbish,* or not? Since we were
in different alphabetical sections I only spoke to him once
in a while during school hours. It was at Roscoe's that we
formally met. He was a *loco* boy and knew the area well.
I guess this gave him confidence in dealing with bars
and other locations that we went to. He was also openly
sarcastic and quick witted. We hit it off though, and found
common ground in a great many things. He told me he was
an excellent piano player, which turned out to be true; he
was much, much better than I (Keith Emerson and Rick
Wakeman were his keyboard heroes). He had been a top
student at his parochial school; he participated in sports,
namely soccer, and was a good darts player. He was in
pharmacy college because he loved science. He also liked

to party a bit, well, maybe a lot. So far, so good. But his
initial claim to fame was as a great foosball player. He even
wore a shirt that proclaimed: Foosball Wizard. He got me
on that one. I couldn't play at all when I started college and
marveled at his intricate ball movements on the bar tables
we played on. He wore a glove when he played and sprayed
silicone on the rods. What a connoisseur. He would always
complain that the beat up bar tables were not as good as the
one at his house. He indeed had one, I played on it once
and it was spotless and correctly balanced. Other foosball
players in our class stepped forward as the year wore on
and some became better than he. One fellow in our class,
T.F., was virtually unstoppable while playing the front. I
learned quickly and in short order also became a threat to
the school's hierarchy of the little white ball. "Hurricane or
Million Dollar" became our elitist shout outs when entering
a drinking establishment to play local chumps. Both types
of tables had slightly different men, surfaces and balls.
Roscoe's had a Hurricane table but the Million Dollar one
was the official "tournament" model. We didn't care. We
just loved to play. A quarter got you a spot on the table,
eleven balls and a game. It was fun. The Foosball Wizard
and I started out as, some would say, dueling antagonists.
We were similar in so many ways that classmates thought
we were in constant competition with each other. Not true.
We partied together a lot over the years, shot darts, studied

together and liked each other's company. By senior year we were finally roommates. The Smallman and the Foosball Wizard lived together! The dart games and throwing star feuds were outrageous fun. The notorious after-dinner bong hits let us keep our "cool" when stressed. Our foosball doubles matches were a riot, sometimes staying on Roscoe's table unbeaten for hours on some nights. I never had a better male roommate in those five years. Sure there were a few bumps during our tenure together but the ending was smooth and the parting joyful. I had gotten into dental school, he into a medicinal chemistry doctoral graduate program. Both the Smallman and the Foosball Wizard would go from talented and bizarrely smart party animals to successful professionals. He called me Putz; I called him B. We communicate to this day.

16

Pledging vs. G.D.I.

G. D. I. stood for God Damn Independent, and I was one of them, or independent like "them." Whatever. In other words, I didn't belong to a fraternity or sorority. I was nobody's *brother* or *sister*. I never wanted to be left alone, just LET alone. However, as soon as college started, out came the frat brothers and sisters, hounding we frosh at every turn. We got hit on right out of the gate. In the cafeteria, in the student union, at parties, in the bathrooms, etc. Nothing and no space were sacred. I resisted all the untoward overtures and outright lies to join "benevolent" and "necessary" groups of men. The sense of belonging to something larger than oneself was the overriding theme and many freshmen succumbed to that fable. In some fraternities, pledging was truly hell, having to wear weird clothing to classes, straw hats, make-up, and carry lunch pails to be raided at will by older *brothers*. There were at least four active fraternities on campus. You know, the unpopular and forgotten one, the nerdy goody-goody one,

47

the popular "rambunctious" one, etc. The lone sorority was more demure, secretive and not as outlandish in its hazing of female initiates. But they were all lame and useless to me. Our college put up with the inhumanity of male rush week and it was soon over. The new frat boys got their pictures added to the "esteemed" photos of fraternity alumni already lining the college halls, and they received perks such as old exams and insider information. However, what seemed like a noble and righteous thing to do back in the day, morphed into irrelevance in the present. I have asked countless former fraternity members if they still kept in touch, paid annual dues, partied and shared friendships with each other? You know the answers. Of course they didn't! I'm glad I never capitulated and sold my soul to a bogus higher power. I had all the same old tests, partied with whomever I chose, and never dated a *sister*. I was proud to be a G.D.I. then, and still am.

17

Care Package Dining

I hated to be fussed over in that way. But that's what my
mom did to me, anyway. But she was right, you know. As I
had never even boiled water growing up in my chauvinistic
household, how was I going to survive on my own? The
pharmacy college cafeteria closed in the early afternoon;
the whole damn college was closed by 5 p.m.! What about
the eats? Where and how? And money? By good fortune
my first landlord had agreed to cook dinners for me and
my best pal from high school if we bought the food or
gave him money, whichever. However, my mom still sent
me prepared, frozen provisions, either through friends or
through regular personal weekend visits. She didn't want her
freshman boy to go hungry! I could never say no to familiar
home cooked meals, ready to heat up and devour. It caused
a bit of embarrassment on my part having to stack the
limited freezer space with my goodies. And, it made me look
cheap in front of my new friends that witnessed me *noshing*
on home-made goods, such as Estonian pirogies, instead of

eating Big Dom's pizzas and subs. But these were extra food staples, in addition to the nourishing dinners provided by the landlord, that first year away from home. I survived, my parents were happy that I was not getting thin, and none of my buddies teased me. Of course, I came to find out later that most of them also participated in care package dining to some extent. Now, we know. By fourth year I started to be fed by my future wife. However, I didn't just stick my snout in her feeding trough and inhale slops. She was a clever culinary magician and brought me up right, much to my mother's chagrin. Sorry Mom.

18

The Pharmacy Finger Curl

You could always tell a pharmacy student from others in
a crowded bar by the way she/he held a beer bottle. Yes, it
was that easy. Sometimes, just to do something offbeat and
completely different, we guys would venture into "other"
drinking establishments around the local area. And, there
were many to be found. Although not quite England,
with a pub on every corner, our town also had its share of
watering holes. The Pheasant Pub, the Legg Room, Mama's,
Groucho's, and our own "pharmacy bar" Roscoe's, come to
mind. And these were all within walking distances of most
of our apartments. During the first week of school, freshmen
year, it was *religiously* instilled upon us in Inorganic
Chemistry lab to NOT drop any expensive glassware.
Tucking the pinky finger under every piece of equipment
prevented slippage and breakage. We were hapless and
sometimes hopeless neophyte pharmacy students and needed
all the help we could get. And that "rule" really helped
us all. By midyear, no one was dropping or demolishing

anything in that chemistry laboratory. The professor was happy and we felt exclusive. Although dancing around with yucky and slimy chemicals, nothing fell out of our hands anymore. This translated to the bar scene, as well. None of us dropped any bottles or glasses of beer either. One quick glance in a "foreign" bar quickly identified pharmacy college students. We checked out their hands first, then boobs, if they were women. Of course at Roscoe's everyone's pinky was curled under a beverage, as expected. I still do it to this day, and unconsciously, whenever someone hands me a nice, tall, frosty one. What a useful habit to have.

19

Kaiser, Part II

F. and I had moved to a huge Victorian on South Main Avenue, complete with the same landlord and his dog. Two more housemates were added. Now there were five of us plus a large canine, all male, all living under one enormous roof. But why would I devote two vignettes to a dog? Because he was that special. At least I thought so. A few stories back I discussed my first unplanned and trepidation-filled meeting. Now, to continue the *tail*. Kaiser was an oversized, black colored German shepherd, with white markings on his chest and belly, but with ears and a tail too large to be a show dog. He was big, mean, protective, smart, and always menacing. However once he gave you the nod of approval, you could do no wrong with him. The landlord always kept him inside except for the usual call of nature walks he took him for in the backyard. This dog hated mailmen, kids, other dogs and cats. We all thought this was normal and he was bluffing until his multiple clever escapes out of the house manifested in two bitten mailmen, a shredded

mailbag, one bitten child and a dead neighbor's dog which
he had cleverly chased into oncoming traffic, only to stop
short himself. There were lawsuits, all dismissed, and
he wasn't euthanized. The landlord used us as absentee
witnesses. "Kaiser never bit me or any of my pharmacy
student renters, Your Honor," the landlord would plead
time and again. This was true, and he always got a reprieve.
Kind of like Marmaduke in the comic strip. However, we
had heard of some cash payments that were made under
the table to disgruntled neighbors. Anyhow, the dog lived.
Although frequently "guilty," he was always acquitted! Our
front door had a large plate-glass window in it. Whenever
someone came to the door, you know what transpired:
Kaiser would extend his body full length, put both front
feet on the window sill and bark his head off. There was a
Windex bottle on the floor in the hallway to wipe the dog
spittle off the window once the barking ceased; we all took
turns wiping that damn glass. It was a very frightening
and intimidating sight. I'm sure many would-be salesmen/
saleswomen and possibly crooks probably jumped off that
porch, missing steps in between, just to get away from that
Animal! But he loved us and knew the difference between
friend and foe. We had parties, we had tons of people over
at Action Central. Anyone that got past his barking got the
sniff test and, if we were not in danger, they could pass. We
all loved him. He wasn't very cuddly but accepted the token

petting as a hazard of living with humans. He slept alone on the carpeted, second floor landing and before curling up for the night would check on each of us in turn to make sure we were OK. Many nights as I sat up late studying physics problems and organic chemistry equations and mechanisms, he would gently nudge open my door, look at me, snuffle a bit, back away, and go to the next room. He was the sheriff and had to make his rounds. He just had to. Kaiser did have an Achilles heel, which the landlord revealed to us early on, just in case we had a real problem with him. He hated the sight of the canister vacuum cleaner and its noise, especially the noise. Whenever things got a little testy with a visiting friend or we wanted him moved out of a particular area, just making the "vroom" sound sent him packing in a panic. He would bolt for shelter in the attic, quivering and whining all the way. It was his Kryptonite and we were careful not to abuse this knowledge. He was an integral part of Action Central and was probably saddened to see us depart. However, new boys joined the house thereby giving him perpetual guard duty, which he evidently loved. He was a unique character, although only a dog.

20

The Police, Cars, and Boston

Yes, it's a misleading title and no, I was never in trouble with the fuzz in Massachusetts. I didn't even have an automobile, yet. Those were the names of some of my favorite rock bands at the time, and I still enjoy listening to them. I'm kind of stuck in a time warp; the '70s rock scene had a profound effect on me even though I was a classically trained pianist. I sucked as a musician, although I could play the piano and violin respectably back in the day. Anyhow, my best friend and I unpacked all our vinyl records and used his hand-me-down turntable, receiver and speakers to blast out the tunes from Action Central. As was the custom in those college days, the speakers pointed outward from his bedroom window, to annoy the populace with rock-and-roll and show off a little. We were college boys, dammit, and that was our sound! Boston was and is my favorite band. They must have really struck a power chord with me. In addition, The Cars, The Police, Styxx, Queen, YES, Billy Joel, Van Halen, ELP, ELO, Led Zep...

were other groups that I loved to hear out. The list could be
exhaustive. And I also dabbled in the harder stuff, such as
Black Sabbath, Judas Priest, Iron Maiden, Triumph, Rush,
Motörhead and AC/DC. Why not? Our live-in landlord
was a church cantor and gifted organist but tolerated our
"music" without saying a word. Our *smart* roommate P.
liked a milder and jazzier form of rock, and Johnson loved
the *Saturday Night Fever* soundtrack and that glitzy brand
of jive hogwash called disco. Even though we four freshmen
didn't exactly share identical tastes in tunage, we never
usurped each other and got along. Our musical interests ran
a long gamut at Action Central. Even I enjoyed some easy
listening to Bread, Firefall and Carole King at melancholy
and homesick times. I don't know what my former
apartment dwellers are listening to these days; I'm still
mired in the muck of the late seventies and early eighties. I
recently had the opportunity to attend a Boston concert at
a small local arena with my wife. The crowd was older, well,
elderly-looking, like me, darn it! Oh, well. Brad Delp is no
longer with us but Tom Scholz was still energetic and, with
a new lead singer, the old sound was still there. And the
band took me home that night, with more than a feeling…

21

Nicknames

Oh, boy. It didn't take long to happen, at least with me. My last name managed to flummox most of my freshmen pharmacy class as it had done previously in high school. Enter the same ole' nickname: Putz. For various reasons no one could accurately pronounce Mayputz with a straight face. So "Putz" became my official name for the five years of college, Smallman, the unofficial one. Even faculty members referred to me by the former. I didn't mind, I was used to it, regardless of its connotation. And, God forbid, no one called me by my first name; Isadore, or Izzy. My other identity, Smallman, was basically a third-person reference name and rarely used outside of my personal cadre of chumps. But to be fair, lots of men in my class quickly garnered nicknames, as if a right of passage into college. Curiously, the womenfolk did not have the same burdensome affectations. We called the girls by their real first names and usually received a positive response. Nevertheless, the ladies got the memo early, most certainly rolled their eyes, but referred to we dumbass *boyz* by our new nicknames. It was interesting to witness all the concerned and surprised faces of my fellow classmates upon hearing my full name pronounced properly at our graduation ceremonies. It made me laugh. Some of my closest friends didn't know my complete name, or how to say it: Isadore Schaghticoke Mayputz! However, I'm not in Hollywood, and have no plans on changing it. I'll just be a "Putz" forever, I guess.

22

Fatso's

I should have known that the discotheques springing up all over our college town were harbingers of the pretentious dance craze sweeping across the U.S. As freshmen we were invited and driven to those "party halls" for special occasions put on by fraternities and/or sororities. The annual Halloween party was one such festivity. Fatso's was a huge warehouse-type building with multiple dance floors, live D.J.s, flashing lights, multiple bars and *swag*. It had a reputation as THE place to go for disco dancing and hookups. It was open seven days a week, and the purported throbbing music and strobe lights never ceased to entertain. The ulterior motives of the frats were to gain recruits. What better way than to rent out Fatso's, ply the ignorant with liquor under the guise of a party, and then get them to promise to pledge. Sometimes it worked, sometimes not. Of course we first-year patsies didn't pay for the booze or any cover charges because we were subsidized; but the regulars did. Other new "dance" establishments in the area were similar: shake 'em down,

pack 'em in and let 'em dance. I had an okay time at that
Halloween social, didn't let any sleazy frat brother cozy up
to me, and was not a dancing fool at the end of the night.
I never went there again. I hated the music, the contrived
convivial atmosphere and, besides, I didn't have a car. Well,
disco started dying and Fatso's folded during my five-year
sentence, and was converted to a furniture store. Good
riddance. But I know some of my classmates, including
Johnson, really missed the place. His five-inch tall, pink-
colored platform shoes would now be relegated to the back
of his closet, right next to the sequined, white bell-bottoms,
neatly folded on the floor. Hey, like today's hip-hop and rap
crap, some imbeciles actually liked that rot from the '70s.

23

Student Union Ping-Pong

While packing for college I included my table tennis bat, not only because I excelled in the sport but to remind myself of home. My old man, a former state table tennis champion back in the old days of the sport, taught me the game, in our poorly lit and low-ceilinged cellar. We had a decent table and played regularly in the wintertime. There were no indoor tennis courts where I was from, tennis, my main sport, was relegated to three seasons only. Pops and I pounded that small white ball every winter, on almost every snowy night during my high school career. We both used Stiga paddles with Yasaka Mark V rubber and Halex three-star balls, all top of the line equipment back in the '70s. None of my high school buddies could touch me in the sport. I thought I was in heaven when I entered the pharmacy college student union center for the first time and saw upperclassmen smacking a ball around at high speeds on the table in the center of the room. This college might be okay, after all. The cramped and dingy

expanse was in the cellar, underneath the dingy cafeteria.
It boasted two broken vending machines, a pool table with
a missing cue ball, a dilapidated but functional generic
foosball table, some chairs, tables and a Ping-Pong table,
complete with worn out and shitty racquets. Oh, and one
scuffed up and crappy Sportcraft Ping-Pong ball. I was
a freshman and had only been in school one day when
I decided to try my luck against the older guys. Girls
didn't play. I unzipped my special paddle pouch, took
out a Halex ball, unbuttoned my shirt, and assumed an
offensive posture behind the table. My opposing senior,
who fancied himself a *player* laughed hysterically as did a
bunch of onlookers. Though I was a little shy back then,
I was relatively confident when it came to table tennis.
Well, I spanked him. I doubt he saw the ball whiz by him
at times. A small crowd had gathered towards the end of
the game and marveled at my proper technique and skill.
I must have grown an inch from all the compliments
I received. I was one proud freshman. However, no
one wanted to play me after that outburst of talent.
Nevertheless, word soon spread and a fellow classmate,
whom I shall call Brian, challenged me. He also removed
his bat from a special leather container and appreciated
the quality of ball I used. Uh, oh. This guy was probably
trouble. And he was. Although not possessing an orthodox
swing or form, his game was very effective against me.

We had many battles and were probably even in the win
column. People would gather round whenever we showed
up for a showdown. It was a spectacle of contrasting styles.
We usually put on a good performance, with trash talking,
diving for balls, offensive lobs and quick smashes when
necessary. We both worked up a sweat and had to change
into spare shirts before going to our next classes or labs.
It got to the point where we only played each other. No
one else wanted a piece of us. When we appeared, even
upperclassmen would vacate the table, sit down respectfully
and watch how the game should be played. We ended
up playing less and less as the years went by due to
girlfriends, class load and lack of desire. Once in a while,
however, we would crank it up and light up the dimly lit
student union with our matches. The game has changed
dramatically, however. The balls are now also yellow and
20 percent larger. The scoring is different, and the paddles
are more expensive. I still play and currently utilize a
Killerspin Diamond TC carbon-wood bat with Butterfly
Catapult black and red rubbers and Chinese DHS or
Japanese Butterfly Olympic balls. I have my own table,
in my high ceilinged finished basement. I sporadically
play in a sanctioned local table tennis league and do well
against the other men, and some women. It's fun. Just one
aside: Back in that dreadfully stressful freshman English
class, we had to do a "demonstrative" speech, as one of

many different types. I talked about table tennis and how
to correctly play the sport. It was the only A I received
all year in that damn course. I guess I knew what I was
talking about, perhaps because everyone else, including the
obstinate professor, was clueless. Except for Brian, that is,
but he wasn't grading me!

24

The Usual Suspects

Every class had them; every school and college, for that matter. You know who I mean. The gunners, cutthroats and backstabbers that feigned scholastic ignorance and professed their idiocy at every chance. Meanwhile, your GPA was going south, theirs– upward! The old sandbag routine. Well, it didn't take long for us "regular" clods to realize we were purposely and maliciously being hornswoggled by a few distinct classmates. I had no problems with honest to goodness intelligent kids that aced tests, studied hard and were proud of it. Nevertheless, I couldn't stomach the two-faced finks that desperately wanted to fit in with us "cool" guys, all the while secretly conniving and keeping their brown noses to the proverbial grindstone. It's hard to lead a double life. Some of those shills even went so far as to appear woefully dumb and inept in the classroom by asking the professors inane and often insane sounding questions. My posse just wanted to beat on them in those instances. One guy in particular thought he had "us" rolled until I finally called him out, in front of witnesses, about his "mysterious" lack of party attendances and indulgences (smoking dope and drinking alcohol). He first professed party piety, then grew belligerent, then finally threatened to punch me if I didn't shut up. I had that short-statured hobbit and his uni-brow twitching in anger. Good. But nobody talked to the Smallman like that, especially with my party cred, and surrounded by my allies no less! He left the scene and we all laughed. I knew it. He was one of "them" and never showed up at one of our parties again. Good riddance to that fake. But why were those certain students willing to keep up this ruse? Were they really fooling anyone? Was it a clever psychological gambit, to get the rest of us off our games? One girl in my class really irked me to no end. The endless dumb-ass questions, the clueless faltering of her voice, the frequently puzzled expression on her pretty muzzle. Her long, bottle-blond locks softened her appearance somewhat and belied her steely internal resolve of getting ahead at all cost. Of course she eventually was admitted to the exclusive Rho Chi Pharmacy College Honor Society; of course she went on to become a doctor; of course she did! It was annoying witnessing those personality types at work all around us on a daily basis but we saw through their mental monkeyshines after a while and it didn't bother us as much. However, no one liked to be duped to feel sorry for someone unnecessarily. Well, that's my rant against those jerks that tried to jerk us around all those years ago. And, you know, I met a similar bunch of phonies during my dental school education, years later. But this time I was prepared and I did "them" one better, frequently beating "them" at their own games. Purposely spreading disinformation, withholding old exams, intentional needling, and talking shit to those rat-fink bastards was exhilarating. Nothing gave me more satisfaction than hoodwinking and snookering those sniveling bullshit artists. I loved it! But did I end up becoming one of them? Did the bullied become the bully? Nah. I only trod on the deserving scurvy lot and hopefully left an honest footprint and legacy among most of my fellow dental graduates– let's hope.

25

Old Exams

Everyone "in the know" had them; it was no secret. Freshmen, including myself, frequently and shamelessly ingratiated ourselves to anyone possessing those golden papers of GPA-raising knowledge. Obtaining, studying and memorizing old tests/answers was a necessary evil but a time-honored pursuit at our fine institution. Even the "brainy" types of students bragged about having them. I personally made an effort to procure as many as possible, in all courses, if feasible. Oftentimes that was a time-consuming and monumental task in itself. However, sometimes it was better to search than to study, especially when it came to Biology and Biochemistry, for instance. Woe to the "honest" student with integrity that only studied and did not use old exams to prepare for a test. The joke was frequently on that student. He/she often learned the hard way, by failure. Many lazy profs actually reused old test questions year after year. Others, not so much. Of course, once in a while a professor would awaken from his/her soporific doldrums and *maliciously* write new test questions. That would upset the "system" greatly, and the current students, as well. My future wife and, her class in particular, was often the victim of this kind of underhanded chicanery. The nerve of some professors! As the years went by, most students had amassed huge quantities of old tests and openly shared them with underclassmen; we were all in this pharmaceutical quagmire together. A few cutthroat connivers hoarded theirs, but everyone still had access to those coveted exams of yesteryear, if you knew whom to ask. A big shout out for old examinations and the corresponding correct answer keys. I know I was greatly helped, and I have integrity, I think. Maybe.

26

The Zoology Term Paper

I had received an 87(B+) final average in Botany the first
semester and was seriously threatening to score an A- in
Zoology, the next semester course; both taught by the same
kooky entomology professor. The same guy that would
annually appear in a raincoat on the last day of class and
allow students to pelt him with insults and water balloons.
Anyhow, I was on the cusp all semester, flirting with the
90 mark. A required five-page term paper, on any animal,
was coming due soon and I decided to write mine about my
dear old friend, the praying mantis. I was somewhat of an
amateur naturalist, with knowledge about most common
insects. As a youngster, having reared hundreds of mantids
gave me confidence to write about this particular arthropod.
What better way to impress an entomologist than with an
entomological discourse on a major insect. All my other
classmates purposely and wisely steered clear of a six-legged
topic for fear of ridicule and being unjustly graded by an
expert. I took my chances. I hated to be a brown nose but I

really wanted that A. I had gotten close in Botany and was
pissed at myself for falling short. No more Mr. Nice Guy.
I had to go all out, or all in, for this paper. I had about a
month's worth of preparation for it to gather facts, figures
and sources. It had to follow strict guidelines and be a
legitimately worthy college term paper. All sources had to
be quoted and numbered accurately, proper footnotes used,
and with the necessary bibliography attached to the last
page. Wow, it proved to be a daunting task; first to hunt and
gather, then scribble down some factoids longhand, and then
to type the damn thing! The wacky prof did not tell us what
percentage of our final grade this paper would count for. I
didn't care. I wanted to impress him with my entomological
acumen. I also remembered that he had frequently given
me compliments during the tedious laboratory sessions,
and high marks for the required pictorial lab journal. Those
drawings of observed flora and fauna were a large part of
the lab grade for Botany and now Zoology, as well. I had
decided to definitely include a drawing of a mantid for my
paper. It was not required, but what the hell? My other first-
year classes suffered because of my sudden deviation from
them and devotion to a darn term paper. I wrote it quickly
enough, plugged in the required references and quotations,
and then spent a few days on the cover art. Well, the project
took longer than expected; I had to share my landlord's
heavyweight '50s era Smith Corona typewriter with my other

three roommates, who were also writing their brains out
and needed to finish. The weekend before it was due turned
into a madhouse at Action Central. The normally placid and
smoky atmosphere deteriorated into ugly squabbling over
worn out black typing ribbons, Liquid Paper correction fluid,
and over usage of the overheated MANUAL typewriter.
It's a good thing my mother had suggested I take typing in
my senior year in high school. Though a little rusty, it only
took me a few hours of pounding those stiff keys to finish
my labors. I redid the cover drawing, stapled the mini-
masterpiece together, and went to bed at 2 a.m. Monday
morning, while still hearing the clacking and cursing of
my roommates outside my room. Six hours later, that same
Monday morning, we handed in our sweat-soaked papers, at
8 a.m., in the Bio lab. All that extra effort on my part proved
to be well worth it. Although my paper was crisscrossed
with red ink, and although the cover drawing was also
decimated and bleeding red, the prof evidently appreciated
my "freshman" effort and gave me an unequivocal A. My
roommates and most others in my class received Cs. The
goofy prof did scrawl a modicum of praise in the lower
right hand corner of my last page, "Brave effort, maybe
entomology for you?" I laughed. My paper had sucked as a
piece of scientific writing but apparently was good enough
for an A when compared to the other pieces of soiled toilet
paper handed in. I received a 93 (A) final average in Zoology

but an 89 overall Bio grade for the year, which included the previous Botany average. I was greatly disappointed because an 89 equated to a B+ and deflated my fragile GPA. However, I had keenly proved to myself that I could come through when necessary, if I really had to, I guess. The kindly but often bewildered professor and I remained on friendly terms for years and I would periodically visit him, make leg room for myself between hundreds of his empty glass Coke bottles, and chat about all things buggy. I think he appreciated kibitzing with a like-minded soul. He was a confirmed teetotaler, but what a *trip* he was.

27

Saturn

I never wanted to be a real rocker, but that fanciful thought did creep into my cranium, at times. It would often happen at a live-band mixer, as I wishfully listened to the keyboardist fingering his instrument. I had taken obligatory piano lessons for thirteen years, received perfect scores at four NYSSMA piano competitions, had given a butt-load of recitals at my hometown churches and halls, and reached grade 5 level music. So why didn't I have a garage band, or still play? Because while I could read and memorize notes, I was NOT musical. I couldn't improvise, couldn't write melodies and could not play by ear. I was tone deaf; I was a good piano technician but a very poor musician. There were, however, a few "real" musicians and singer song-writers in my pharmacy college. Each class seemed to harbor at least one, sometimes secretly. Some even used alias names when they performed. The "music meister" in my freshman class was a *mensch,* though. P.L. was a friendly local boy, with a local non pharmacy college girlfriend. He had a band called Saturn since his high school days, and used his real name onstage. He didn't care. And he played the ivories, too. Although P.L. was an ardent YES fan, he and his band mates would instead play the easy rock genre of the day. Nothing too complicated and definitely no prog-rock. They occasionally played for our mixers, for weddings, bar mitzvahs, etc. You know, local gigs for a few bucks, here and there. As usual, the band changed personnel and its name, going from Saturn to Uranus, and then finally to Raven, before disbanding during my third year. As frosh, lots of we classmates would trudge out to watch and hear P.L. in action. Remember, he was one of our own. He didn't disappoint and always opened the first set with a lyrical song entitled *Aimee*, by Pure Prairie League; his one and only lead vocal. Once, however, a female singer and classmate named R., a guitarist who was also my *smart* roommate P., and I were surprisingly asked to perform as a light-rock trio at a fraternity function, with the dean of the college in attendance. In addition to the slow stuff, we also had the opportunity to play a few songs from P.'s favorite bands, Little Feat and Duke Jupiter. It went okay; we each got a free gefilte fish dinner as payment. Yum. And it was my last time attempting to emulate Elton John and his musicianship. And Saturn? I wished I had been a member but they already had someone tinkling the keys named P.L., and I had no real talent. Oh, well: memories.

28

The Boys Back Home

There we were, ready for some prime time action, with the female kind, that is. But were we really ready? I mean *really?* Probably not. Most of the prettiest freshmen girls had steady boyfriends back home; at least that's what they told us. And to be honest, most of us "men-boys" could not supplant their mates from home anyway, at least not as acne-faced and bumbling frosh. Initially, we had nothing going for us. We needed time to season and mature before we could try to pry those women from their manly roots. We also needed part-time jobs, cars and decent haircuts. Those were hard things to get, man! What girl in her right mind would just give it up to a nerdy freshman when she had a *real* man back home? Not many, I surmised. And for some of the females, this trend continued for all five years. A few of our pharmacy sisters even became engaged to and married their *home bois* before graduation day. We just couldn't break some of them, no matter how hard we tried. We also believed that this unattainable feminine beauty was wasted on what we guys regarded as inferior men. It made us angry and unappreciated. The Italian women took the cake, however. Sure we dorks were immature, poor, etc. but when we compared ourselves to the fellows they brought to pharmacy parties, we had to scratch our heads and wonder. Come on. Those guys? We were going to be pharmacists; what were they going to be, brain surgeons? I doubted it. However, we did admire the loyalty of those fancy princesses. They never wavered and stuck to Vinny, Nick, Tony and Guido like glue. Hey, who am I to ridicule or admonish? I got over my anger, my jealousy, and gained a girlfriend during my freshman first semester. It didn't work out but, hey, that's life. Nevertheless, speaking as a perceived anti-feminist, those Italian girls sure were good looking; what a waste...

29

Bambu' vs. E-Z Wider

Darn it. Just when I thought I had the rolling part down
pat, now came the choice of paper. Nothing was ever easy.
There was lots of gossamer-thin papyrus to choose from but
the two most common brands at the time were Bambu' and
E-Z Wider. Over one hundred different types are available
today, with various sizes, thicknesses and flavors. Some
are even mentholated; most are constructed for cigarette
smokers. Nevertheless, we basically bought the two popular
kinds: Bambu' and E-Z Wider. Both were commonplace
fixtures and advertised packs could easily be purchased at
convenience stores, gas stations and Head shops. Most, if not
all, rolling papers are still manufactured from "rag fibers,"
found in non-woody plants such as sisal, hemp, rice and flax.
Each company's secretive fabrication process determines the
slowness and evenness of burn. The thinness, handling and
sealer also contributes to the reputation of each brand. For
us, Bambu' was the gold standard. An old Spanish lineage,
that firm originally produced bibles, then retooled itself for

a more lucrative venture: "burning" tissue paper production. The company philosophy probably remained intact, however, since the "new" paper was also for the HEAD. Bambu' was expensive compared to its contemporaries and boasted a natural African acacia tree gum sealer; this was one fine paper. Delicate, strong and tasteless; when you mentioned Bambu', talking Heads nodded. Belgian-made E-Z Wider was also widespread. Its claim to fame was ease of use. Being slightly thicker than Bambu's paper, it tore less frequently and was ideal for beginners. It used high quality, natural gum arabic for its sealer. E-Z Wider was our staple paper. Of course, most partiers already came with rolled bones; there were no brand names emblazoned on them. It was hard to tell the difference between papers, especially in dim, smoky rooms. Although sometimes a proud purveyor would announce the paper used, if it was expensive, just to get some stoned adulation from the stoners. I personally liked to mix it up, purposely, of course. I'd whip out an all-American made Zig Zag rolling paper packet and brag to onlookers that I only used American products— which was untrue— as I deftly and expertly rolled a blunt, before blazing up. The awe-struck and dumbfounded expressions on the panic-stricken faces of my fellow devotees were worth my temerity! However, I've been out of the loop for eons, now. But with many states legalizing weed consumption, I'm sure that there are even more choices of paper available for today's already fucked up hipsters and old hippies to roll.

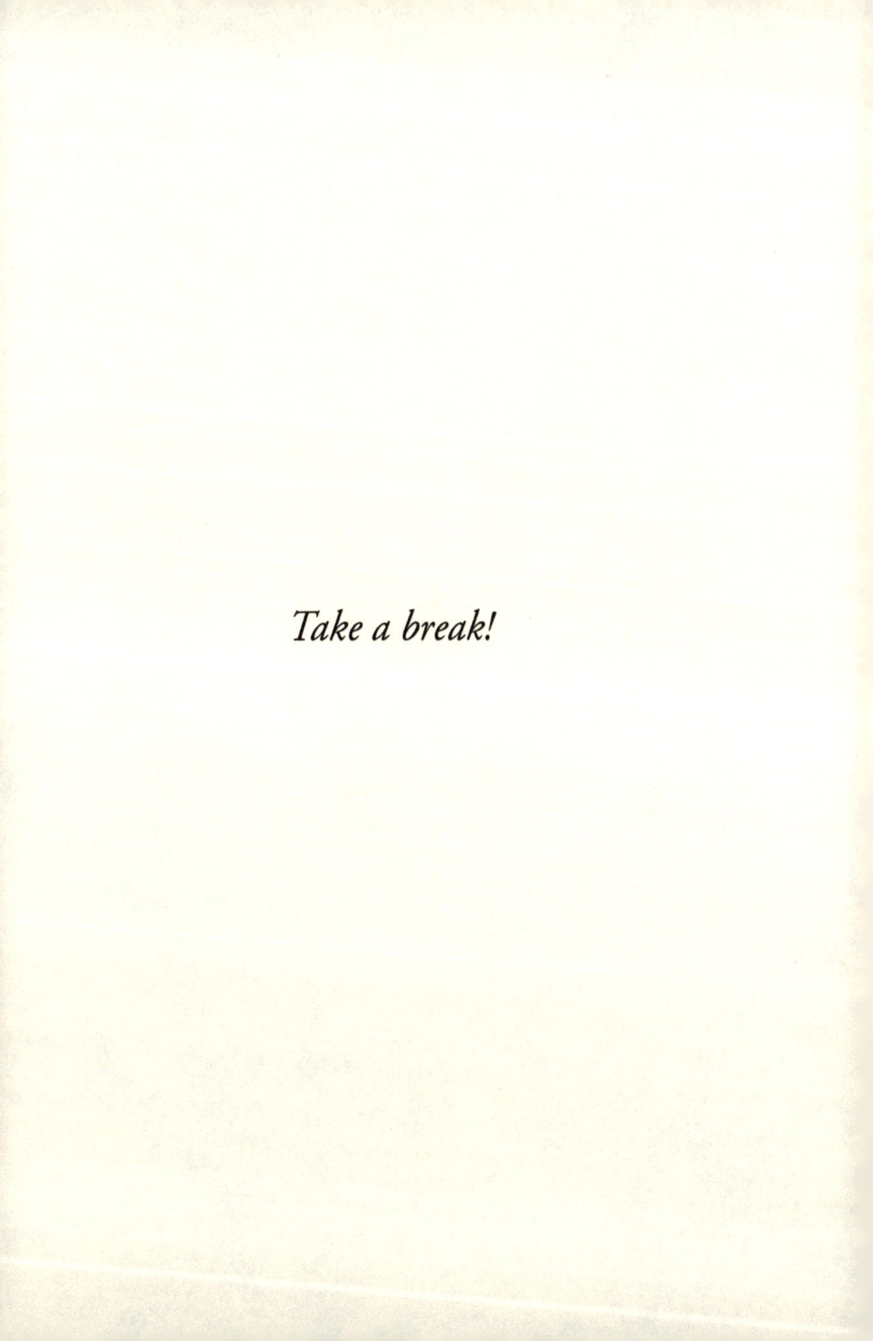
Take a break!

SECOND YEAR

30

Johnson

He was part of Action Central, and then again he wasn't.
He was a trusted fellow housemate; then again he wasn't.
He exuded many personalities from his mind but was not
really a bad fellow, or schizophrenic. He was basically a
good egg who thought a fake persona was what he needed
to project in order to be liked by all, especially women.
He was smart, always well dressed, well coiffed and always
SEEMED cool. He even combed his thick mustache daily,
with a special comb. But he never let his guard down, even
for a second. Well, what better target to aim at than this
two-faced phony. We three roommates quickly saw through
him and it was a no brainer to tease the shit out of him,
to at least make him respond in an honest way. We had to
do it. It was for his own good, I thought. He never dated
anyone from our school, and held court with women, like
the Fonz did, in distant bars, and fancied himself a disco
impresario. Whenever we invited him to Roscoe's to party
with us, he always agreed to come but never showed up.

And when it came to sparking up some doobs, he was
nowhere to be found. Looking back now, perhaps we
rock-and-rollers were mean and crossed the red line many
times in our pursuit of "righteousness" and humor. He
took it stoically instead of lashing out and pummeling us.
I mean, he was a great athlete, bigger and stronger than
any of us, but chose the high road time and again. But
the more he ignored our taunts and elaborate schemes, the
more we persisted in our ribbing of him. Hell, he was part
of Action Central, dammit, and we still couldn't resist.
What the heck was wrong with us? What the heck was
wrong with him? We three nicknamed him Johnson and
we stuck to it, behind his back of course. Other friends
immediately knew whom we were discussing or plotting
against once that name was mentioned. It was code for
horseplay at Action Central with Johnson being the patsy.
I won't bore you intellectual readers with the extensive
list of infantile and most sophomoric pranks we put him
through those first two years of college. Well, maybe just
a few examples, when we thoroughly bushwhacked him.
One of us substituted Tide detergent for foot powder in his
dresser drawer. We were all walking to school in the rain
one morning when his Converse sneakers, the ones with
the two holes on the sides, started to blow bubbles with
every step. We three conspirators burst out laughing as he
squished and squashed. He wasn't amused. Or, the time

one of us left his pajama bottoms draped over his bed with
a banana forming a tent in an inappropriate place, knowing
that he was bringing a date over. The screaming girl called
him a pervert and quickly left our house. He was not
amused. The mashed potatoes in the slippers and pizza in
the toes of his cowboy boots were mild compared to the
drinking glass episode. Someone taped a clear fishing line
to the back of his plastic drinking glass which he already
had in place on his immaculate desk. The other end was
looped under the desk and tied to his chair. Of course,
when he pulled the chair out to sit down, water splashed
all over his homework and ruined his deeply prized
desktop cover. He swore that was the last straw. But it
wasn't. Not even close. Okay, four more and that's enough.
Someone kept putting small cardboard wedges under the
two bedposts at his feet. Over the course of a few weeks,
he complained that he seemed to always get a head rush
whenever he went to sleep. His discovery of said prank
cracked us up. He was not pleased. Someone carefully
removed his triple locked authentically autographed
baseball from its protective plastic display case and lightly
penciled in a fake name on the back of the ball. One day
he was showing the baseball to a would-be girlfriend when
she remarked out loud, "Who was Dick Hertz, a pitcher, or
catcher?" Once again, he was mortified. Someone carefully
unpacked his stash of Q-Tips and marked one side with

yellow marker. He confided to us later that he became extremely angry thinking he was using soiled tips in his ears. He almost returned them back to the pharmacy where he bought them. We roared. One of the last classic episodes of tomfoolery involved his birthday, a cake and his would-be date. The girl had brought over a handmade Bundt cake covered in aluminum foil and one of us had her put it on his desk and we promised to guard it until he came home from a bike ride. Things went awfully awry when two of our stoned buddies arrived, prior to we three departing for Roscoe's. P.M. stared at that giant aluminum "ball" on Johnson's desk. I told him to keep moving and pay no attention to it. But no, he insisted on checking it out. "Was it Jiffy Pop popcorn?" he slurred. We three started to panic. Let's get those trashed fellas out of his room before something gets irrevocably wrecked. Too late. One of those whacked out pals, P.M., suddenly and capriciously smashed the cake with his hand, leaving rather detailed impressions of his fingers in the aluminum foil. We gasped. Crap, and we were supposed to protect that cake at all cost! We quickly left his room and tried to leave the house but Johnson and the girl who brought the cake arrived at that same moment. I quietly told the guilty party to scoot out the back door and he did. The girl started to cry and Johnson nearly blew his top. We weren't laughing because we weren't really guilty. Each of us in turn proved to him that it was not our hands that did it. The imprint didn't fit any of us. He was perplexed and we played dumb. Someone must have broken into the house while we were in it just to smash your cake, we chimed in. Yeah, that must have been it. You must have many enemies, or jealous women, we told him. Maybe the landlord came down from his attic abode and did it. I mean, he hated chocolate. Maybe Kaiser, our German shepherd did it? We even tested his right paw in the imprint; nope. The girl left in tears and Johnson finally broke down. Perhaps he had real feelings after all. Perhaps his distrust of us was justified and we did him wrong all this time. Maybe it was time to grow up and stop this nonsense. After all, he was our buddy and fellow Action Central stud, and we liked him, to a point. We really weren't bullies, or were we? We stopped the bullshit and he was grateful. Well, we promised to stop until the second year ended. But that didn't include the last day of school, we told him. He laughed and then scowled in panic.

31

A.P.s?

It was early second year when I found out that maybe, just maybe, I wasn't as dumb as I thought. I had struggled in freshman calculus, suffered and sweated through first-year chemistry and wasn't exactly acing sophomore physics early on in the semester. How could whole swaths of my second-year fellow students seem to "get" stuff so easily? Were they really that much more intelligent than I? One evening, P., my *smart* Action Central roomie, "accidentally" revealed that he had previously taken a slew of A.P. courses in high school, including biology, calculus, chemistry, English, and physics. I didn't know what he was talking about! What did the initials A.P. even mean? Advanced Placement, that's what. My boffo high school, in Bumfuck, N.Y., had only offered advanced courses in animal husbandry and metal shop. We had regents and non-regents classes; that's all. It finally dawned on me why I felt so "behind" certain classmates. They had a leg up on me, those dirty dogs. They had learned those subjects

before; it was a repeat performance for them. I felt cheated
but morally and mentally vindicated. Now I knew what
A.P. actually stood for: <u>A</u> _Putz_; me!

32

Bandanna Man

It was yet another usual Thursday night at Roscoe's that fall: Bud splits (four for a dollar), quarters lined up on the Hurricane foosball table (it cost a quarter per game), no elbow room, and the distinctive squawking of the Space Invaders video game in the distance. There was also the usual paucity of women present. What else was new? But hold on there, a stranger appeared among us, not seen before by us regulars. He held a beer bottle without the "pharmacy pinky" curled underneath; he looked troubled, was gaunt and tall, and had a swarthy complexion. He casually put a quarter on the foosball table to notch his turn and nonchalantly waited. He was a townie, scary looking, and had a red bandanna tied around his right wrist. Was he a gang member of some sort or did he venture into a pharmacy bar just to show us dweeby college boys how to play? He had no partner when it was his turn at the table. He muttered and motioned at the existing winning team to play him two on one. He must be really good I thought. We were all wary of him; nobody bothered with introductions as play began. This was going to be some serious foosball. Well, he sucked. His awkward, spastic movements around the table looked like Joe Cocker singing. He frequently bent the rules by spinning his five-man rod and actually bent the goalie rod many times in frustration after missed blocks. No one said a word as he "convulsed" on his side of the table. He almost always lost, stomped away angrily but kept returning to put up yet another quarter. He carried on as if foosball was his passion in life. He appeared and disappeared on most Thursdays for years, sometimes winning a few games against girls but mostly losing to the men. We had some talented players in our school (including me) that became better as the years went by. We relished *showing him the door* early in the evening. No matter, he would just cough up more quarters to play again and again. We never did learn his identity or why he frequented "our" bar. By fifth year he was showing up on sporadic Thursdays and still losing most games. He had become a fixture in our lives, a story line. We made him out to be a surly character, an outsider, an outlaw. But he must have had a real life outside of Roscoe's, or did he?

33

J. B. Scowles

My first introduction to this bad boy of bars was in the
autumn of my second year. It had a sordid reputation as
a loud and obnoxious night club; not for dancing, not
for womanizing but for hard drinking and hearing loss.
Hearing loss? That's right. Hard rock and heavy metal
bands were the featured artists on most nights. None of
that silly disco stuff there. It was located right on a main
drag avenue and a few minutes walk from our college. We
didn't go there at night although I passed by it many times
in daylight hours. However, it looked as though it could be
a rough place, pleasing a rough crowd. I obviously didn't
belong there. I surmised that the drinks were probably
expensive and the cover charge steep to keep the large
venue going, and to pay the bands a few nickels. Anyway,
a tall, brawny, and long-haired freshman roommate of my
friend D. was scheduled to open there for Judas Priest on
an upcoming Saturday night. What? Now I personally
knew this Peter Frampton lookalike, having already visited

D.'s notorious "party" apartment numerous times. A. was quiet, studious, respectful of the Smallman and a decent chap. Not some stuck-up punk rocker that always wore shades. He was the unlikely frontman for a local hard-edged metal-band named Fury. I don't recall if he had joined them while still in high school or was a recent addition. Of course, I had never heard of Fury either. None of us had. So, after vowing never to set foot into that tawdry cesspool called J. B. Scowles, I and a small herd of male sophomore pharmacy students made our way on a rainy Saturday night to see A. perform. I was a Priest fan but would not have gone if it wasn't for A. playing there. Plus, there would be a requisite pricey cover charge. After being proofed, we all got in and took seats near the back of the joint. It was still early and some tattooed Harley babes were finishing up shooting pool in front of the stage. Tough-looking bouncers patrolled the large bar area and gave us menacing looks. This was definitely not Roscoe's! It was nine o'clock and we were ready to rock. As advertised, Fury took the stage with A. grabbing the *mike* and looking every bit a legitimate rock god. He borrowed a "Bic Flick" lighter from an adoring chick offstage and let loose a fiery gas plume from his mouth, all pre-planned and staged. We were enthralled, excited, and, with our pie-holes open, in disbelief. The four-piece band cranked some chords and then launched into a hard-version cover of *Sister Seagull*, by

Be Bop Deluxe. A. strutted and sang, and strutted some
more. He was a seasoned pro at this game, it appeared.
My mind quickly compared another local band, Saturn,
to Fury. Not even close. Fury was certainly an appropriate
namesake. Twenty minutes later A. was offstage, drinking
beer, and relaxing with us at our table, ready for Judas
Priest to come on. We all congratulated him and just sat
around, staring at him in awe; and he was just a freshman
at our school. By now the place was mobbed with many
unsavory characters surrounding us. We held our ground
and our table, barely. There were some unpleasant glares
in our direction, but nothing happened, probably because
A. was in our midst. Rob Halford of Priest came roaring
on stage on a hog, and started right in with his four
band-mates. They were an up and coming mega group
that was still playing small clubs at the time. Well, I
hung around for a few songs, started going deaf, quickly
decided to call it a night, and walked out. A few other
classmates and some regular patrons joined me in exiting
the building. The show was just too damn loud for such a
small place. Fortunately, my hearing returned the next day.
On Monday at school, my *home boyz* and I rehashed the
thrilling previous Saturday night and commented on the
outstanding showmanship and singing of A. And he still
wanted to be a pharmacist? What was wrong with him? I
never went to J. B. Scowles again. But as a music/bar joint,

it lasted long after many discotheques of that time era had bitten the dust. A. graduated as a pharmacist, changed his name and started a successful solo singing career. It made sense. I wonder though if he ever quit his day job?

34

Sexual English?

After my debacle with freshman English, I looked forward immensely to the second year English course taught by the portly Prof. N., that emphasized reading and writing. That's all. I could do that, I thought. The class curriculum was basically reading a set of well-known books by major-league authors, discussing their literary merits, and then writing essays about each one. Very simple, but you still had to know how to read and write; you couldn't just fake your way through that class. Of course Cliff Notes helped, but Prof. N. knew that many students used them and devised devious exam questions that forced we lazy asses to READ THE BOOKS. However, a curious classroom phenomenon seemed to occur with each book we read. Prof. N. nonchalantly but regularly "discovered" sexy content in every book, and then expounded on it. Some books were so bereft of emotionalism that we were always amazed by his implicit and explicit pronouncements of shenanigans between characters. Did he have a special "teacher's" edition he was reading from?

He would interpret the slightest titillating phrasing or a vague adjective as a full blown sexual situation in the most mundane of chapters. Maybe he did it to get our attention or perhaps just to spice up a dull read and a dull classroom. However, it was fun to witness his apoplectic gyrations and sputtering at the lectern while explaining a perceived bit of naughtiness to us. Even the female students would roll their eyes and smile. We all loved him. I did very well in his class and always alluded to sex, as needed, on all my exam papers. He also taught a third year elective called The Novel, which my future wife took. She would later tell me that it was more of the same; a continuation of second year English, with "sex" springing up from the unlikeliest of places in novels that were plainly devoid of any obvious nooky. Such was his genius. RIP professor N.

35

Mixing It Up

This story could easily have been titled Inter-school dating, but that wouldn't have been accurate; it was such a rarity. We mostly partied with, doted on, and dated our fellow classmates. But once in a while we adventurous men and ladies would step out of our comfort zones and attend mixers held at neighboring colleges. Sometimes we went with our significant others, as well. Most of these socials hired decent sounding local bands, had a nominal cover charge and were legit parties, sanctioned and often sponsored by their respective universities. They were also held in large venues around town such as in the Knights of Pythias and Knights of Columbus halls. They were PG-rated affairs, with dancing, good rock-and-roll music and cheap beer on tap. But we X-rated and horny teen-aged pharmacy males always kept an eye out for that "special" someone to hit on. What can I say? I was also guilty of that habit. And I even had a current pharmacy college girlfriend. However, nothing happened in the boy-meets-

102

girl department. Not even one-night stands, as far as I can
remember. At least not with any of my immediate chums,
or myself. But, anyway, I was taken by a pharmacy girl at
the time. Women from the other colleges were intriguing,
talkative (after a few beers) and frequently attractive, but
we kept going back to our own. I'm not sure why that
happened. Familiarity seemed to breed sex, not contempt.
And I often wondered how we doofuses appeared to those
"foreign" females. I probably know the answer. Now,
when the medical and law schools had their mixers, many
pharmacy college females attended and tried to mix it up
with those perceived "alpha males." I'm sure some succeeded
in getting noticed; whether it led to more dates is hard to
say. My "un-steady" girlfriend eventually left me for a law
student by the middle of our third year. Who knows how it
happened? But by the end of my third year I ended up with
another *home girl*, a fellow pharmacy student two years my
junior, that I eventually married. But those mixers had been
a blast, a carefree and sexually anticipatory time for those
few hours at night, away from the rigorous pressures of
organic chemistry and physics. It had been fun and exciting.
I sometimes miss those *knights*.

36

Jefferson Park

By our second year, most of my pharmacy college compadres
started to become braver with their surroundings. And
that included me. Living away from home had its good
and bad points. The same went for not having dorms.
However, learning to pay your own bills, rent, do your own
cooking, cleaning and laundry just plain sucked. Anyway,
one thing we were warned about as freshmen was to STAY
AWAY from the unlit local parks, especially at night. There
could be undesirable bums, villains and killers lurking in
the shrubbery. This official school bulletin was especially
impressed upon the ladies. So here's what really happened, in
a nut shell: Crocked and staggering college students, and not
just from the pharmacy school, would come pouring out of
Roscoe's and other bars after midnight and disperse through
the streets like hobos on the run. No one paid any heed as
to where she/he was not supposed to trespass. In a drunken
state, all that you wanted to do was get home and crash out.
So you walked through a forbidden park, big fuckin' deal. Or,

was it? In the day time, the parks were gorgeous; some even had tennis courts where I played. But at nightfall, a different story? Jefferson Park was directly in the path between Roscoe's and Action Central. Sure, you could go around it and waste twenty extra minutes, or you could man up, hold your breath and quickly walk through it. I rarely drank more than I could handle and could sprint rather quickly if I had to. Therefore, crossing that "menacing" stretch of alleged banditry was so makeable for me. My roommates did the same. Unfortunately, the pharmacy girls also followed suit. But nothing untoward happened to ANY pharmacy student that had to step through that nighttime nightmare. At least not during my second year, and that I knew of. Now on one occasion I was walking home through there alone, after 1 a.m., and physically ran into a partially undressed clergyman. Even in the dim lighting I could make out the white holy collar around his neck. I heard some rustling in the bushes next to him and footsteps running away from us. I just kept my head down and persisted in making hasty tracks. I "saw nothing." I wasn't a good witness; I didn't want to be one. I got home okay and told my buddies the sleazy story. They weren't surprised. After my second year, though, I didn't have to march through there anymore. I had moved to new lodgings and it was now just a dark memory. Hopefully the town tramps also stayed away, unless they wanted a prayer service or some other kind of "offering" from "Father Pantless."

37

The Evil Twins

They hit us low and they hit us hard. And I'm not talking about opposing football players. I'm referring to those infernal fraternal basic science twins: Organic Chemistry and Physics. Although obviously non-identical, they shared similar adjectives such as anguishing, painful, outrageous, egregious, and stultifying. And those are not just throwaway words to dress up this vignette. Those dueling dragons of disaster were in fact second-year science courses that actively sought to separate the weak from the strong. Anyway, that's the perception that was duly impressed upon we frightened freshmen. And it worked. As second year began, my housing situation became stabilized at Action Central, I had a steady girlfriend, and I felt ready to tackle school; and I mean really tackle it. My freshman year had been spotty and lackluster at best, marred by unacceptably low final grades in English and Inorganic Chemistry. But this was a new year, a new start, a fresh step for me. The Smallman would not disappoint this year, damn it. I was ready. Both courses were taught by elderly professors looking to dial it in, and get the hell out of that hellhole called Pharmacy College. However, if you possessed a good memory and memorized the heck out of old exams, you could easily score a high grade in both classes. And if you handed in your lab work on time and pretended to know what you were doing during the lab sessions, you were golden, too. "Cheese" was the nickname of the Organic prof. He was stout, pugnacious and absurdly loud. And he had a habit of drawing endless organic "mechanisms" in chalk all over the blackboard. Most of us bored students reluctantly gazed at them, often with glazed over stares. It was a tough class to comprehend. Nothing really made any chemical sense, at least not to me. The Organic Laboratory portion was also a nightmare scenario, with open jugs of volatile, flammable, and noxious liquids haphazardly arranged in non functioning and slimed-up laminar flow hoods. Toxic fumes were probably ever present in the air but we were too stupid or ignorant to realize it at the time. Where was OSHA, the EPA, HIPAA, the DEA, PETA, the ASPCA, etc.? No one came to our rescue. Hanging above the office door in the lab was a large maroon banner with yellow-colored, crossed shaft sticks on it and with the following words emblazoned underneath them: Never Give The Student An Even Break. Was it a joke, or not? We did experiments while standing underneath that damn banner and promptly left that lab as quickly as possible. Physics was a similar animal. The lecture portion was a non-stop deluge of banal and inapplicable formulas presented by an overhead projector onto a screen in the front of the lecture hall, room #404, next to the stinky cafeteria. The boorish and pontificating professor had a healthy disdain for we dummies and frequently lectured us on our poor behavior and test performances. Fortunately, my lab partner in the Physics Lab was one of our brightest students, C.H. He made the labs look easy. We were always done first and always scored A's on the complicated but lame lab experiments. Thank you C.H. I hope you are happy, successful and satisfied as a know-it-all clinical pharmacist, somewhere. You really were smart. And me? I memorized my notes, the old exams and aced the class tests and labs and was rewarded with solid A's in both Organic and Physics. Winning! By better budgeting my time and partying only as necessary, I seriously thought I had hit my stride that year and cockily imagined myself as a chemistry whiz. Boy, how wrong I was. The following year would bring me down to earth, and then some. However, second year had been marginally enjoyable. It was refreshing to at least get one good year under my pharmaceutical belt, so to speak. However, I started to feel mentally and physically worn down near the end. But I had actually made the Dean's List twice that year, both semesters!

38

Psych Center Frisbee

Well, we had to play somewhere. Somewhere local, with a large lighted area, in a safe neighborhood, and at night! Oftentimes, after studying our asses off before major exams and then having a few cold ones, a few of my athletically inclined buds and I would meander over to the well-lit, and well-groomed grassy grounds of the local psychiatric center. No one would bother us as we tossed around a few discs. Cops on night patrol probably saw us throwing those "pie plates" at one another and they did nothing. We really didn't break any rules, there were no signs forbidding Frisbee playing at midnight on Partridge Street. Once in a while a white-clad "inmate" would join us. We didn't care; he tossed a good Frisbee! We didn't cause a scene or a ruckus; we played for a while, laughed a little and went to our respective apartments to get some shuteye prior to the exam the next day. Who said that we always behaved rudely and crudely? Who said we couldn't have some honest and clean fun? Of course we

were careful not to let any of the uncool pharmacy crowd
actually see us without booze and bongs in our hands. We
had our reputations to uphold, you know.

39

Drunk as a Skunk

I was at Roscoe's when it happened. It was a wintry Thursday night and I was still sober, playing foosball, winning and losing. It was a typical night after studying. Since the college locked its doors at 5 p.m. Roscoe's became our defacto student union in the evenings. And on Thursday's, drinks were half price for the ladies. Some of the opposite sex from our school actually ventured into this dive, this "unofficially" sanctioned pharmacy bar. I was standing around, watching my quarter go up on the foosball table, waiting my turn to play when J.S. burst through the back door and rushed over to me. He was one of my close buds and I turned to him. He was out of breath, mussed-up, sweat-soaked in his goose-down coat, and rambling on about P., my *smart* roommate from Action Central. Then he grabbed me and my coat and physically escorted me out to his parked, faux wood-paneled, red-colored Ford Pinto wagon (death trap), in front of the bar. What about my quarter? Oh, well. Outside, he proceeded to tell me that P. was in serious trouble on Hacket

Boulevard. "What kind of trouble," I asked, somewhat jokingly. J.S. was not kidding and looked deadly serious. I quickly realized something was really wrong. We drove about ten minutes and then spied P.'s car, an old, early '60s, light blue Oldsmobile, that burned oil like a bastard. But it still ran. The car was parked in front of an apartment complex where a small and impromptu girls' pharmacy party had just disbanded. J.S. and I peered into the car and found P. slumped over and passed out, and appearing quite ill. We banged, we tried to open the doors, all to no avail. Perhaps we should have called the fuzz? Nah, then we might all get in trouble. A man passed out in his car and two other guys slamming on it trying to get him out. What would the cops think? The situation did not look promising and the outside temperature was dropping. After a few anguishing minutes, P. stirred, just enough to reach up and manually unlock the driver's side door. J.S. and I dragged him out, threw him into the back seat of the Pinto and took off. We had locked his car, of course. We sped to Action Central and quickly enlisted the help of Johnson and F. to bring P. into the house. He looked in rough shape and couldn't speak. Then the dry heaves started, what a mess. J.S. told us that he and P. were having a good time with the womenfolk at that party and planned on going to Roscoe's afterwards, to meet up with me. But P. had one or two too many, and was now lying prone on the cold stone foyer floor with Kaiser whining over him. Shit, we weren't doctors, what were we going to do next? Maybe take him to the local hospital; call the ambulance? Wake the landlord? He was sleeping upstairs in his attic apartment. What could he do? It must have been acute alcohol intoxication, we geniuses surmised. So we carried P. up to his bedroom, plopped him belly down on his bed and left him there. J.S. drove to his place and we three went to bed. The next morning, there was no sound of life emanating from P.'s room. I cracked the door open to find he had puked dark brown bile all over his white sheets and, he was still fully clothed from the night before. He was face down and hadn't moved a muscle all night. The landlord was apprised of the dire situation and promised to check in on him during the day while we three were at school. We came home that Friday afternoon to find P. had at least changed his body position on the bed but could not be awakened, try as we might. He was not drinking water or able to eat. There was a hushed silence at Action Central, almost like a vigil for a dying hospice resident. Saturday night came and the landlord had promised us a dinner. As we three roommates sullenly took our seats around the dining room table, we heard rustling and someone coming down the stairs. It wasn't Kaiser, but P., freshly showered and looking embarrassed and out of sorts. He sat down with a thud and we all breathed a huge sigh of relief. He remembered very little so we proceeded to boisterously fill him in on his hiatus from the living. He could now walk, talk and eat but appeared a bit wobbly. But he recovered quickly though, cleaned up his room, apologized to all that had helped him, thanked J.S. and me personally for "rescuing" him and walked over to pick up his car. He was fortunate that his car keys were in his pants pocket and not stuck in the ignition. He drove his old jalopy to Action Central and slowly regained his senses. And, you know, he became *smarter* than ever in the ensuing years. That alcohol had not damaged a single one of his brain cells. Or at least he had a vast reserve that the rest of us did not. In hindsight, we had acted stupidly and negligently. We should have hospitalized P. right away that night. He would have prudently been put on I.V.'s, had the appropriate critical care and perhaps recovered instantly. But we didn't know about health insurance, if his parents would be pissed off or not, if we would somehow be held responsible, etc. He could have died. But we didn't know how serious his condition was or wasn't. P. had gotten lucky. Anyway, we were happy that he was back to "normal." And he didn't repeat that kind of drunken bullshit ever again, as far as I know.

40

The Second Year Skits

The Second Year Skits was an annual student performance that showcased the college's benevolence in "sanctioning" the gentle roasting of professors, other students, the administration and situations at our esteemed pharmacy school. I emphasize the word *gentle*. As freshmen we had attended the Second Year Skits in the school's dilapidated auditorium and I silently vowed not to let OUR year turn in such a lame, inane and tame show. By second year, Action Central had effectively taken charge and started planning this "comedic" extravaganza. The administration minions and wonks figured we knew the drill and had received the memo. You know, keep things professional, but with a sense of high-brow humor. Yeah, right! Like THAT was gonna happen. Instead, I plotted to bring a whole new LOW to the "skits." My high school chum, best friend, and fellow Action Central conspirator joined forces with me, once again. Just like the good old days. F. and I were used to this kind of format, having pulled off many entertainment shows together since ninth grade. We had usually executed pun filled send-ups of popular culture, loosely patterned after Monte Python's Flying Circus, its irreverent blokes and, their zany brand of sketch comedy. We weren't that good but we used original material and got laughs, if only at the high school level. Other interested parties soon joined us to work on the writing, editing, lighting, and acting. F. and I knew all about producing a staged affair, quickly organized the willing and able students, and scheduled the rehearsals. Weeks were spent sporadically practicing, memorizing lines, "working the stage," getting costumes together, etc. It was coming together fine, full of innuendos and low-brow humor. Then one day in physics lab my *brainy* partner C.H. casually informed me that he and two others had a surprise addition to the production. He laughed as he tried to tell me but couldn't. He did ask me to leave a spot open for he and his buddies at the end of the night; I said okay. I mean, any sophomore could contribute, so why not another act? The fateful night finally arrived. F. and I manned the *mike* in turn to introduce the multitude of scenes and actors/actresses. We also took part in some of the horseplay onstage. Fortunately for us, the packed auditorium was mostly *de*composed of raucous, drunk and stoned male students from all years; however even some of the women present were tipsy and disorderly. We continued to skewer professors, students and situations to roaring applause and laughter. So far, so good.

My *smart* roommate P. even did a spot-on imitation of Mr. Rogers and his Dysfunctional Disco Neighborhood, busting on our other roommate, Johnson, the disco dork. The few profs in attendance might have been spies but they were also hysterically nodding their approval. The end of our theatrics was fast approaching and we might have not only gotten away with some of our ribald and inappropriate monkey business but received compliments for them, as well. However, then came C.H.'s turn at the *mike*. He and a friend told the audience that they had just seen the dean of our college arrive and he looked pissed off. Since C.H. was not known as a jokester, the crowd believed him and started to look around and murmur uncomfortably. It was perfectly plausible for the dean to check out HIS college. After all, he ran the *joint*. Even I didn't know what to expect next. C.H. purposely feigned terror on stage as he nervously looked around, pointed and then said, "Here comes the big prick now." Entering from stage right was his third friend, dressed up as a large pink-colored, circumcised penis, complete with wobbly testicles. The workmanship of the cloth outfit was excellent; it could have been used as mascot garb for a seedy sports team. We "seasoned" humorists and actors, including myself, didn't know how to react or what to say. I was stunned into silence. The crowd yelled and clapped; the few professors still present cringed and quickly slunk out the back doors. Many of the heavily bombed howled and whistled their approval at our innovative audacity. Meanwhile, I mentally recoiled, realizing there could be serious repercussions for sinking this time-honored ship. Anyhow, it was embarrassing and damn funny at the same time. The spectacle ended, the curtain closed and the lights came on, thank goodness. People in attendance filed out shaking their heads, some still laughing, some looking puzzled. Was it OK to laugh at the dean that way? But nothing happened to we pranksters, although we did get wind of a "reliable" rumor implying that we had almost scuttled the 100-year-old tradition thanks to our needless and *dirty* antics. However, we weren't banned from school and the Skits went on the following year as usual, although this time the dean came to watch, and the show was indeed PG rated with good, clean, wholesome, respectable jokes and humor. I also attended just to observe; sober, mind you. Boring is what it was; very uninspiring and unimaginative. But, hey, we had previously gotten OUR licks in and were satisfied. And our alleged screw up further cemented Action Central as the college authority on comedy and deviancy, even though C.H. had upstaged us with his big dick.

41

The Normans

I realized that sometimes my comedic overtures took a silly
turn or rudely fell flat. It was inevitable living with two
"cornball" and like-minded fellow pharmacy students at
Action Central. Our fourth roommate, the "serious" one
with a serious mustache, was often present but really didn't
fit in with we jokers. We referred to him as being seriously
silly, behind his back of course. We clowned around a lot
that second year, between intense bouts of studying, partying
and womanizing. Well, I had a steady, so…not so much
for me in the latter department. And oftentimes we would
get unexpected visitors on our stoop, ringing our loud and
obnoxious sounding doorbell. Kaiser, the resident evil, I
mean German shepherd, was usually the solo unwelcoming
committee, jumping up to the door's glass window and
barking his head off at strangers. His threatening tactics
undoubtedly frightened many an unwanted solicitor
from our domicile's steps. Unfortunately, he failed as
an adequate deterrent for the Normans. That was our

facetious name for a religion that makes its worshipers wear magic undergarments. And whose members make regular proselytizing religious pilgrimages to all neighborhoods, including our house on South Main Avenue. Always well attired and groomed, the pious parasites, usually men and sometimes women, would patiently stand on the porch until Kaiser tired and gave up barking. One of we weisenheimers would finally grab Kaiser by his collar, reluctantly open the front door, step back and, annoyingly start listening to the rehearsed spiritual dogma. Our politeness usually ended after a few agonizing minutes of that phony baloney and we would curtly and abruptly slam the door shut. Kaiser would always look up at one of us with a disappointed face, as if to say, "Damn, why couldn't I put the bite on them, just a little nip?" But they must have known we were just goofy college students devoid of any faith. Perhaps that's why they kept on coming, like locusts, to convert us. They were on a mission from God, we were godless missionaries of stylized depravity. To each his own. Nevertheless, those "social" calls finally ended. P., the *smart* roommate, once actually let three, black clad stooges, enter our foyer while restraining Kaiser. I happened to be coming around the corner from the dining room to go upstairs but stopped to eyeball the holy trinity. One of them smiled when he saw a bunch of empty metal coat hangers draped over the banister near the bottom step and asked what they were doing there. I glanced at the

Normans, grabbed a hanger and nonchalantly said, "That's for the abortion clinic upstairs." There was some shrieking and lots of pushing and shoving to get out. And they were gone, never to return to our supposed heathenish den of inequity. P. just stood there, mouth open, eyes unblinking and stared at me in horror and disbelief. "Why did you say that?" he implored. "It wasn't necessary," he admonished. In the heat of the comic moment I admit I may have panicked and probably crossed the line. I apologized profusely to P. for fear of having possibly violated his theological leanings, if any. Then I saw a sly smirk cross his face. Darn it, he got me! We both burst out laughing. And the Jehovah's Witnesses? That story will NOT be retold in this book.

42

Insider Trading

I was walking down one of our college's main halls at
noon, on a Friday, when I heard, "Hey, Smallman, I got
something for you." I turned and saw H., with his locker
open, and beckoning me toward him. The hallway was
deserted; we were alone. I smiled as I briskly approached
a fellow crony. Of course the Smallman was friends with
many students, but H. and I went back to his freshman
year when I had given him some timely old exams and, it
seemed, he was grateful. Maybe he had a gift for me, or
something? We spoke in an easy jargon that only the *cool*
kids understood. We stood there nodding and laughing.
He reached deep into his locker and quickly placed two
aluminum-wrapped cubes into my hand. I nodded in
approval, but before I could exit stage left, we heard a loud
voice near us say, "Gee, Putz, I didn't know you gambled
in school?" What? The second year "class nerd," C., had
come out of nowhere and saw the whole thing go down.
He thought the silvery cubes were dice, and assumed that

]

I was a hard core gambling addict, and even gambled in
school! Craps! He walked away smiling as if he finally
had something over on me. H. and I laughed haltingly
but quickly parted company. He slammed shut his locker
door and bolted for the staircase. I slowly walked away
after pocketing the "dice." Well, it didn't take long for
some of my classmates to inquire about my shooting dice
habit, etc. It was a big laugher, sort of. And C. suddenly
fancied himself a funnyman, a punster. He swore that he
saw the Smallman gambling in school. I said nothing. My
buds knew the real story. We had the last laugh when we
pinned up, lit the contents of the cubes, and inhaled deeply.
Even though that nerd tried to sully my name, which was
impossible, he was alright. He was an "original" and not
a dastardly transfer student. Though somewhat squirrely,
he did finish second in our class and eventually became
a stalwart professor at our alma mater. Maybe I should
contact him and reveal the true essence of that long ago
fateful meeting when he became a big shot for a day.
Maybe I'll send a copy of this book to him. Maybe.

43

Quarterlies

Every college on a two-semester system probably has them. You know, the exams that were given at the halfway mark of the first semester, one quarter of the way through the school year. At our college, however, even the second semester midterms and all finals were colloquially called Quarterlies. The word became synonymous for a week-long examination period and hell week for pharmacy students. Each day of that week tested a different course, with each test usually lasting three to four hours. The mere mention of the word Quarterly brought visions of fear, apprehension and anxiety to an already mostly studious, angst-ridden, and nerdy crowd. To top off this serious drain of brain power, they were held in the college's old-fashioned auditorium, which also doubled as a gymnasium in the late 1800s. Different class years had their Quarterlies at differing times, but only that dang auditorium was used as the place of execution. Hard wooden desk/chair combos, a hard wooden floor, dark purple curtains, and no ventilation was the crime scene description at that depressing and merciless testing ground of students. It was sparse, brutal and no nonsense, as if to further foist that feeling of gravitas on us. I don't think we needed any more stress or piling on but I wasn't the one in charge. On multiple layered shelves surrounding the periphery of the essentially functionless auditorium were giant formaldehyde and alcohol filled dusty glass jars with an assortment of weird, gross, and bizarre specimens floating inside. They were old relics of a bygone era, but our school had a predisposition for revering ancient times and reminding students of the uniqueness of our institution. One time I opened up my Physics test packet, looked up, and saw a damn dead fetal piglet just staring back at me. I never sat near a window shelf again. Sheep's brains, roundworms, giant leeches, human intestines, etc., bobbed about all around us. No one ever complained or became sick and tired of this display; we were all too nervous to get skeeved out. The auditorium was seldom used for anything other than Quarterlies and the once yearly traditional Second Year Skits. There was a grand piano in the corner; no one ever played it, however. And the NEW gymnasium, dug out in 1902 under the auditorium, was where the basketball team practiced and played. Well, that's how we took our lumps and those dreaded major exams back then. Hopefully, today's pharmacy students are appreciative of the cutting edge technology probably employed during their examinations, in air-conditioned rooms, with desks for left-handers and, with the ability to take bathroom and water breaks. Let's hope.

44

Beauty Bomb-Out

What the hell did we *men* think was going to happen?
We drove to a free beauty pageant transpiring at a swanky
downtown venue, all decked out and all lacking girlfriends.
Well, I technically had one but it was more out than in,
if you know what I mean. We were ready for some action;
really? Five of us were on the scene, four from our *frat
house* called Action Central and a fifth tag-along buddy.
We looked good, smelled good and felt good. Bring on the
babes! This was actually some sort of New York State minor
league beauty pageant for B-lookers. No A-1 bombshells
here. We didn't care. There were gorgeous young women
all around us, about our ages, and we had commandeered
front row seats, close to the stage. Reliable sources had told
us that there would be a meet and greet session afterwards.
Hey, did anyone book a hotel room? Shit, no. Well, how was
this evening going to go down, then? Probably in fantasy
land for us naïve blokes! We talked, we schmoozed, we tried
hard. The pretty women wanted no part of us, or parts of

us either, for that matter. Even the open bar didn't help get them undressed. It was a big failure for us. Little did we know about pageant rules, curfews, contestant guardians and parents. We wasted a good Saturday evening being teased by this lot when we could have enjoyed ourselves more at Roscoe's, our familiar pharmacy bar. But it was an experience nonetheless. However, one unfortunate event that DID happen was when P. (the *smart* one from our house) stumbled into a metal door jam and vertically split open his right eyebrow. There was blood running down his face as if he were a boxer; we told concerned onlookers that he had a bloody nose and quickly ushered him into a nearby men's room to get him cleaned up. He didn't know what hit him, being so crocked and all. Thank goodness for alcohol. No doctor, no stitches, just a wet wad of toilet paper for the cut. And by Monday, we boys from Action Central had done it again: we contributed more grist and gossip for our mostly gullible pharmacy brethren. "Did you at least get any numbers?" some of the sapless and wimpy male students inquired? We stayed quiet. Nothing had happened; we just kept smiling as if something had.

45

Blackboard Correspondence

We had no cell phones. And the one and only student messages bulletin board was always filled up with administrative bull crap and propaganda clippings. OK, occasionally there appeared some notices for student ski trips, fun outings and other wholesome activities. But what about party notifications? You know, the actual *meat* of having a good time. Not the college-contrived "fun" that often turned out to be lame. The administrative trolls viciously tore down any postings of frivolous tomfoolery, such as private parties, from that lone message board. And it was supposed to be used by students, for students, "they" told us. Yeah, right. Everything was scrutinized by the "political correctness police," even in those dark ages. So how did we communicate? Blackboards, baby. As freshmen we frequently witnessed older students, female and male, quickly and quietly leaving large lecture halls just before our whole class would file in. We would quickly scan the blackboard and read the address, time and date of a party to be given. Usually the professor would erase it but some decent teachers would actually point it out and make light of it. Well, by second year, our own class became quite adept at leaving those often funny and cryptic chalky announcements in the upper right hand corner of class blackboards. Other class years had their own spots. It was a great way to communicate and infuriate the higher-ups at the same time. We didn't need to text or sext back then. We read the blackboards, attended the parties, and sometimes got lucky, all the old-fashioned way.

46

The Breakup

I guess it was inevitable. It's part of growing up: coupling, parting, changing, maturing, exploring new feelings and relationships. The long-running bromance with my best friend from high school ended rather abruptly, with nary a whimper, in May, at the end of second year. He came to my room that spring evening and whispered that he would be living with other pharmacy guys the following fall. Then he silently slunk back to his room and closed the door. I was dumbstruck. And, just like that, it was over. Our special bond and our *frat house* called Action Central were now mutually defunct. Two important things in my life—kaput. But it was a common story. We had been the best of pals since seventh grade, sharing lunches, sports, books, music, theater productions and a love of Monty Python sketches. We had had nearly identical grades in high school and intact nuclear families. We were a team and had looked forward to living together as pharmacy college students. Nevertheless, subtle cracks started to appear in our concrete friendship by the middle of second year, when things were actually going smoothly, scholastically and socially. Anyhow, my friend started to hang out with a more sedate and laid back bunch, and I with an edgier crew, willing to push some boundaries now and then. For two college years we cooked and ate together in the evenings with our other roommates at Action Central, shared jokes, joints, and jibes; even rode home together to our small village at times, to visit our folks. Our respective sets of parents are still close friends to this day. What happened to us? There were no fights, no spats over women, no nothing. Maybe that was it: no more spark. Was it a gradual cleavage that just kept growing over time (I like how that sounds!)? The summer after the breakup we didn't speak at all, although we only lived 5 miles from one another. How sad. I wasn't angry, perhaps he was? But I was confused. Third year started with us having different roommates and apartments. That autumn we saw each other at college registration and photo ID taking, and sporadically in classes that year. We didn't sit together anymore. Our long-running "comedy act" was officially dead. Thirty-five years have passed since our pharmacy college graduation. We still send each other Christmas cards with the obligatory brag letters tucked inside; we know what each other is doing, how our wives and kids are, etc. However, we've never discussed our breakup; maybe there is no need to. Nevertheless, I believe

it is me that needs closure, not him. I knew him and think
we both lost a bit of self in the dissolution of our union.
But like many great sitcoms with good runs, even they
come to an end. Maybe there weren't any notable nefarious
incidents that happened betwixt us. It might have just been
our time to separate. Or, not?

47

The Last Stand

Custer had his, we had ours. It was bittersweet, to say the least. My two trustworthy roommates, landlord, and Kaiser (German shepherd), minus our recalcitrant cohabitor Johnson, all planned on having a grand send-off to Action Central at the end of second year, the last day of classes to be exact, before finals week. Friends were invited for the early dawn beer bash to commemorate the ending of the year and the ending of us idiots as a fearsome foursome. My best friend F. from high school bailed on me and was going to other lodgings with more soporific roommates. P., the *smart* one, was going to move in with some others he found more suitable; Johnson was staying; and I was going to move in with an unknown but seemingly enthusiastic dude from my class that sought me out, for some reason. We had played foosball together at Roscoe's a few times and exchanged a few syllables and pleasantries, but that was about it. How we got together is still a mystery. Maybe he thought some of my "coolness" would rub off on him? I could have stayed at the

134

dude ranch with Johnson, interviewed two more prospects and kept living there. But I couldn't, I had to move on, it was time. However, first we had to get our party hats on and go out in style! Festering animosities and resentments were squelched for some much needed revelry in those early morning hours. The landlord and his dog, Kaiser, gave us the requisite permission and then quickly sequestered themselves in his attic apartment and let us have at it. Our friends started to arrive at 7 a.m., some were already stoned and blitzed. No women bothered to show up; of course none were invited, not even my then girlfriend. The loud rock music started blaring out of P. and F.'s windows, cases of Pabst and Miller were torn into and the sweet smell of Panama Red permeated the walls of Action Central. It was only 7:30 a.m. dammit and those *boyz* were already swinging from the fire escape! What the hell? All our close buds were there and we were feeling high, and good, too. Someone poured beer into Johnson's bowl of Cheerios without him knowing it. He hurriedly slurped it down as we were literally dancing all around him in the dining room. He just wanted to get the heck out of there and go to school. This was NOT his idea of a "fun" party. We were so immature compared to HIM. I guess. But the Cheerios/beer broth had made him giddy, which he thought was from inhaling all the vaporous hemp fumes. Maybe that, as well. He made a hasty exit, unlocked his ten-speed parked next to the porch, flipped us off with both hands, and mounted his expensive bike. Meanwhile, some of us had gathered on the rooftop outside of P.'s window, armed with water balloons brought by my pal B. We had instinctively known that Johnson would prove himself a heel and we weren't disappointed. The cannonade started raining down on him to many catcalls and derisive remarks. He ducked, swerved and called us names in response. It was all funny until he bolted into traffic to escape that watery barrage and promptly got nailed by a car. Shit. We just stared down at the unreal scene below us. He wasn't hurt; the driver cussed and drove off, but Johnson's getaway bike was mangled, and I mean mangled. We all ran down into the street, stopped traffic (twenty belligerent and intoxicated guys will do that), and started to apologize to him. He was soaked from the bevy of broken water balloons and breathing heavily, but smiling nonetheless. That morning beer must have made him tipsy because he acted like it was all part of the act, a reality show that he was a willing part of. Very strange. F. put the bike's rear wheel between his legs, straightened it as best he could, ripped off the damaged seat and told Johnson to get the hell to school before we really got pissed off at him. The bike wobbled and shook as he tried riding standing up so as not to get a wedgy, and slowly disappeared from view. He looked like a giant circus clown on a fucked-up bike; people stopped and stared. If only he had had a horn. We waved the traffic on, to much cheering from the drivers. It had been

an unlikely improvised comedy routine; everyone seemed
to enjoy it. We slowly sobered up, cleaned up the lawn and
rooftops, the fire escape and bedrooms. We cut the music,
closed the windows, said goodbye to Kaiser, and quite sadly
and quietly started our sojourn to school. No one drove that
morning. It was now 8:30 a.m. So we were going to be a little
late; so what? A wet Johnson had spilled the beans before
we arrived en masse. The "talk" started early that day. Those
guys at Action Central had done it again, one last time; one
last gasp of juvenile horseplay. Many fellow students had
wished they had been there; now it would be college folklore,
past history. Finals came and went and it was time to move
out. It was a turning point of sorts in my young life. "High
School" had finally ended for me. I seemed to have grown
up overnight that last week of school, became more cynical,
and had what I thought was an illness about me that made
me tired. Was it mono? I never found out, but whatever it
was dogged me during that summer and well into third year.
My saintly parents dutifully helped me move once again into
new quarters, in a decent brick building, in a good section of
town, with that new roommate. I went home for the summer,
the new roomie stayed and worked at his pharmacy job. I
sent him rent checks to cover my portion of the rent that
summer. Before I left for home, I did apply half-heartedly for
a part-time job with the local VA hospital, in the pharmacy
department. It was a sought after position; good pay, close

to the school, and a promise to honor a summer internship
there if you worked part time for the entire third year. It was
a good deal but I knew I wasn't going to get it. Too many
applications for a few spots. I was sick, ready to go home and
recover. I had no job waiting for me nor did I want one. And
what happened to that "crazy" landlord of Action Central?
I heard from reliable sources that he followed his "passion,"
moved to Romania and became an ordained orthodox priest.
Of course he was not Romanian and did not speak the
language. Anyhow I always knew he was a strange bird. He
may have flown back to this country by now, for all I know.
Truth is often strange, you know. And Kaiser, that enigmatic
and personality laden German shepherd? He passed away
from cancer a few years after I left Action Central. What
a dog, what a character he was. I was putting some old
pharmacy college books away recently when I saw the Action
Central stamp emblazoned on the binder of Remington's
Pharmaceutical Sciences textbook, our go-to bible back then.
Those were good times, I think.

Take a break!

THIRD YEAR

48

Third Year Funk

A LOT would happen during my third year in pharmacy college, which technically began after second year ended, that May. After the second year finals were over, my parents graciously helped me move to a new place: a two-bedroom swanky apartment on a street called Park Avenue. No kidding. The rent was higher than what my folks paid the previous two years but I would only have one roommate, not three. And no dog. So I set up my room, paid the rent, said goodbye to my new apartment mate, and went home for the summer to rest. I was sick, sick and tired. I hadn't even called my girlfriend, or my former best friend. I was finished with both of them; no more head games. Maybe I was sick in the head? Perhaps. I had applied to the local VA hospital for a part-time job starting in the fall; they promised to answer me in the summertime. I hoped for a positive response, but didn't hold my breath. It was a warm summer in the very late '70s and I was home doing nothing constructive. I went on some lake fishing trips with my grandpa and old man, did some entomological excursions but mostly whiled away the hours wondering if a pharmacy career was still right for me. I had a great second year and all, but I started to doubt if pharmacy was right for me. Was I being premature? I hadn't even yet taken a single pharmacy course. Maybe I was depressed? Maybe I had fibromyalgia or chronic fatigue syndrome? Who knows? A doctor's physical and blood test in June revealed nothing abnormal. What a surprise. In August my family and I made our usual trek to a beachfront camping area in another state. We had gone there many years in a row; it was no longer special but a family tradition. We arrived back home two weeks before third year was to commence. My father no sooner parked our trailer behind the garage when my grandpa (who had stayed home) came running out of the house, yelling at me about some VA dude calling repeatedly in my absence. His broken English notwithstanding, my grandpa had managed to write down the phone number accurately and I started calling. I didn't get the job; I had to go for an interview first. My professor dad didn't start teaching college classes for another two weeks, so I made an interview date and off we went. I stopped to check on my new apartment and then we headed for the VA. I tiredly slumped in a hallway chair and stared at the two others present; another pharmacy student named D. from my class and a young lady. Were we the only *schmoes* present for the interview? I thought the hall would be packed with pharmacy students. Perhaps the higher-ups gave the interviews in shifts? The decked-out dame curtly told us that she was there for the secretarial position. D. and I both joked that we were there to pick up hot secretaries. She wasn't amused, turned on her high heel, and clicked away from us. D. and I laughed, again. I knew this guy, he was also a *cool* customer that liked to party. We had crossed paths at many socials and shared a bone or two in the past. He was also a bit of a wise guy, like me. Dammit, I bet there was only one internship spot available, however. Friends or not, I started to hate my would-be rival. I remember feeling more than lousy that day and suddenly didn't care how the interview would go. I really didn't need the job, it probably would just add to my projected aggravation for the ensuing year. I was almost ready to walk out and join my father, who was patiently waiting for me, but decided not to. I was 19 years old that summer and already in a deep funk. What else could go wrong? And adding to my frustration was the insidious change in musical taste in our country. Disco hit hard that summer, but I definitely did NOT feel like that upbeat song: *Funky Town*! I hated disco, and still do. Third year would be a disaster– and it was, somewhat.

49

The VA Interview

I couldn't quite believe it, sitting in that large, deserted
hallway, about to be interviewed by the Chief of the
Pharmacy Service (not department or section, but service)
for a prestigious (at least by student's standards) part-time
position. However, D., a fellow third-year contemporary
was also there, for the same job as me. Damn him! But
then, much to our mutual surprise, a diminutive black
gentleman in a short, green "VA" tunic quietly came out of
an unmarked door, beckoned us BOTH into his inner office
and told us straightaway to sit down. He was indeed the
Chief, it said so on his oversize and gold-plated name badge.
D. and I glanced at each other and burst out laughing. It
was embarrassing and most inappropriate, but the Chief
had no reaction. He just sat there stone-faced and solemn,
as if expecting this kind of crass shit from us. Two, big,
very long-haired, loutish white dudes were sitting across a
large desk from a short, white-haired, Caucasian-challenged,
polite and bespeckled professional. We must have found the

surreal scene somehow funny. Maybe we were just nervous. He immediately stood up; did he though? I couldn't tell for sure. Anyway, he told us, quite unceremoniously, that we were both hired and shook our hands simultaneously. What? I quickly questioned him about the hiring process as D. made derogatory faces at me. I didn't wish to rock the boat; I just wanted to know what made D. and I so qualified over the hundreds of other student applicants? The Chief confided in us that he was not an alumnus of our pharmacy college and, being rather sequestered at the VA, really knew no one outside his federal pharmacy circles. He went on to say that currently working upperclassmen had unanimously guided him toward D. and I for the two available positions. It's all *who you know,* you know? I guess our school notoriety and selfless sharing of Mary Jane at shindigs had paid off and won us heretofore unknown friends in HIGH places. Bonus! The interview was over in about five minutes. We left his office with high paying part-time jobs (twenty hours per week, some Saturdays, some weeknights). We followed the Chief down the hallway and downstairs to the bowels of the VA, the basement. The dental and pharmacy services were located there, adjacent to each other. The genial Chief handed us over to the black assistant chief, also not from our school. We mingled with the very busy, thirty or so, all-white, male and female pharmacists, techs and secretaries. All congratulated we two "troublemakers." It would be a blast working with a bunch of former alums and older students that actually wanted us there. Third year was about to commence. New lodgings, new roommate, new faces– a veritable avalanche of transfer students– but still the same "illness," same girlfriend problems, harder courses, and now, a part-time job to add to the stressful and toxic mix. Lots of my buddies had part-time jobs at Fay's, Carl's and, even Rite Aid. Plus, my new roommate also worked. If they could pull it off, so could I. Was I ready, though? I was also selected to be a volunteer *disorientation* group leader for incoming freshmen. Maybe that would inspire me to get a grip on myself and continue with this pharmacy *edumication*?

50

Future Hottie?

Who knew? Who knew that the beautiful blonde chick at that seemingly insignificant freshman pharmacy college orientation gathering in the dank and rank student union would one day become my steady, my fiancée, and then my wife. Only in the movies and in real life– mine! I was at that freshman gathering; I was one of a dozen fearless third year upperclassmen who volunteered to be an orientation group leader and show about thirty frosh the school, answer questions, etc. Maybe even be a temporary mentor for some. And that one girl was a true freshman hottie, although she didn't quite look the part, yet. Straight from the boonies of the Adirondacks, she was wearing an oversize, poofy, light blue colored down-coat, although it was about 80 degrees that day. I guess you always have to be prepared when you're a hick from the "sticks." She didn't like my gentle teasing of her over her attire and dour disposition. I mean she just sat there, expressionless, motionless, speechless. Eventually she did volunteer where she was from and sarcastically derided me for picking on her. Only much, much later did she confide in me that at that initial meeting a neighboring freshman girl had whispered to her, "He has a great personality but not much to look at." She countered with, "He's an asshole but is very cute." Looks ended up trumping substance in her mind, and my imprint on her must have been profound. She still reminds me that I was the first actual pharmacy student she met in pharmacy college. Her fellow freshmen didn't count. However, after that fateful meeting, nothing happened. And I mean nothing. I think I heard that she had a boyfriend from back home and I had a steady (yeah, right) girlfriend for the time being. Actually, it was on again and off again with my love life. Nevertheless, I did continually see my future wife in the hallways but had forgotten her name by then. We had no classes together because of our different years and I always seemed to have a girl around, so asking her out was a non starter. But she started to look better and better to me. As she sashayed past us on occasion, my friends would comment on her tight sweaters and good looks. I was mesmerized but still in deep girl trouble. I broke up with the long-timer I had, started up with a new one, dumped her, etc., etc.. What a nutty circus the dating game had become for me. Plus, I had not been feeling well with something like mono (never officially diagnosed) that really dragged me down mentally and physically. I was a messed up, sad case, and ragged out that year. And courses like Anatomy and Physiology, Pharmacy I, and Biochemistry were messin' with me, too. Not to mention Physical Chemistry, which I had cavalierly signed up for as an elective. What a jackass I was; I knew it was an absurdly difficult class and arguably the hardest course in school. What was I thinking? Obviously I wasn't, at the time. All of those third-year subjects were tough-ass classes and not for the faint of heart. And then my thoughts would turn to that mysterious girl. Who was she? On occasion that hot blonde and I would exchange furtive glances in the library and I became enthralled. She had those blue eyes… What was her name, dammit? No one seemed to know. It was rare for upperclassmen to commiserate with underlings, even in the same school and in the same building. There was a hierarchy, a distinct pecking order, and we generally stuck to it. How could I get to really meet her, and when? Well, my health improved near the end of the school year and I shed my latest girlfriend. I finally did get the chance to "officially" meet THAT freshman female muse of mine, and she did become my girlfriend, rather easily, I might add. And she did not disappoint!

51

The Switcheroo

I set the alarm on my Sony clock-radio right after listening to Pat Benatar's new hit single *Hell is for Children* and went to sleep, or so I thought. The alarm radio went off normally, at 7 a.m., to the hideously quacking sound of Disco Duck. WTF? Was I dreaming, still sleeping, hallucinating? *Hell* wasn't for children; it was for me! I fumbled around with the radio, speedily turned the rotary dial to other stations and found the same shit. Disco was everywhere. I turned back to my original station; *Stayin' Alive* by the Bee Gees was screeching at me. It couldn't be. The disc jockey soon came on to say, "Welcome to Disco 101, your dancin' place to be." No, no, no! Not my place to be. What had happened? Overnight most of the local airwaves went from playing Aerosmith to the Village People. I finally dialed up PYX 106; thank goodness they were still playing rock-and-roll. I wasn't going mental, after all. I could have kissed my radio. The rest of that year, disco reigned supreme, much to my disdain and disappointment. I hated it. However, I should have realized that this stupefying and crazy dance craze would be approaching like an incoming lava flow after having attended a few packed "dance" clubs, including Fatso's, as a freshman. Luckily, Americans can be fickle and even intelligent at times; the New Wave music, including The Cars and The Knack, effectively helped douse and wash away the disco inferno gripping the nation. Slowly but surely the radio stations returned to their respective rock roots and my small piece of mind was returned. But it took years to restore "order" and that really tried my patience, and I'm not a patient man. Hey, Donna Summer and Johnson, long live rock-and-roll!

52

The Nephrons

Okay, so I could play table tennis and tennis at high
levels while most of my closest buddies were merely athletic
supporters. You know, fans, not particularly coordinated
or sporty male specimens, so to speak. I was athletically
inclined, so people inferred, but I was totally unprepared
to join a mixed-sex bowling league. I had never bowled in
my life. How would I manage? Why was I asked in the
first place? Well, the annual intramural bowling league
had formed and my new roommate coerced me to join his
team, with two other students that he knew. I went out
with them a few times to "practice." R.W., one of my new
teammates, wore a bowling glove, had his own bowling
shoes, possessed two custom drilled finger-tip balls, and
used talcum powder. I used some dusty old ball I found at
the end of a rack at the far end of the club. I sucked badly
but my bowling partners seemed to hit the pins easily with
those large, heavy, round objects. It turned out that all
three had bowled in high school and were quite good, by

my very limited standards. I had watched PBA bowling on TV and understood the sport but I had virtually no knack for it. I was a fish out of water on the lanes. I didn't know what the arrows were for, if the lanes were oily or dry, how many steps to take, where to stick my thumb, etc. What was I doing with those uncool goofballs anyway? Those *losers* were not my usual posse of friends but I reluctantly agreed to bowl in the league with them. Why not? Maybe it would help me get out of the physical and mental doldrums I was in and to make some new acquaintances. We called ourselves The Nephrons. Why that name? I don't know. We were taking Anatomy and Physiology and were studying kidney function, so perhaps the name sort of came from that? Anyhow, we were officially named and the weekly league began. I didn't realize it at the time but many students that I had dissed and dismissed as not my type were in this league. Some of them regularly hit scores in the 200's and perfect games were not unusual. For me it was almost like joining one of those "anonymous" groups as required therapy. My immediate *smoking* pals laughed their asses off. The Smallman bowling? Ridiculous and preposterous. I didn't really belong, but there I was trying hard to fit in among this crowd of misfits. My third-year roommate and I lived across the street from the bowling alley emporium that would be used for league play. How convenient. Home court advantage, already. Score! We

started out in last place because of me. What I didn't
realize was that poor bowlers got handicap points, based
on their previous average, that were added to the score of
each game bowled. As long as I kept improving, my team
would stand a chance at winning. And that's what started
to happen, and quickly. My average at the end of the season
was an anemic 141, but that was good enough to place us
in the final four tournament. Of course during the course
of the season, whenever we played against weaker teams I
"purposely" bowled below my average. We still won, and
whenever we played against the good teams I tried to bowl
above my average to get those handicap points. It was
a little gamesmanship that all the teams dallied in, and
things turned out fair for all in the end. As there wasn't
much else for pharmacy students to do recreationally as a
large group in the winter, or any time for that matter, the
college therefore readily approved bowling as good clean
fun. It made me gag. Nevertheless, I was amazed at the
attention paid to the standings as the league was ending.
The school administration was also enthusiastic, and really
into it. We four Nephrons became minor celebrities and
were actually talked about by other nerdy and uninspiring
male and female students. How ignoble and embarrassing.
I tried to distance myself from this unique mob of goobers
but could not. Well, we lost in the first playoff round to
the Bark Eaters who went on to win the championship

trophy. The whole school seemed to be caught up in a bowling frenzy that year. It was crazy. We lost, I gained a few more friends I didn't care for but challenged myself to bowl again next year. It had been fun, after all. I returned to the fold of my inner circle and resumed my "normal" decadent ways. However, I secretly plotted to get my own ball, improve my delivery, hone my limited skills, and get a decent hook shot going. And I did.

53

Frustrated Entomologists

Third year was one of transition for me. I was sick, tired, had girlfriend troubles, a new roommate, new lodgings, and a hell of a pharmaceutical schedule. I'm not whining, just stating facts. Second year had been a blessing and a blast, third year, a beast. I suddenly found myself in an apathetic and diseased (unconfirmed) funk that pervaded my personal and scholastic life. I don't know when it started but by the middle of third year I was mentally and physically ill. The courses were okay, hard but manageable. Of course Physical Chemistry was brutal; I was scoring a low C, but besides that I kept my GPA as high as possible. My Mary Jane consumption plummeted and was noticed by my *buds*. They knew something was amiss, as I did, but couldn't put a finger on it. Bong hit after bong hit did not alleviate my mental state of torpor. My new roommate was clueless about my health because we had never lived together before, plus he had a girlfriend and an active part-time job working after school in a pharmacy. He had no time to listen to

my complaints. However, I managed to buck up and kept
going; I was NOT a quitter. My female relationships were
dismal. Rotating between girlfriends was never easy or
satisfying. Although I did encounter a certain outstanding
young, blonde, female underclassman on a regular basis in
school; she seemed familiar, but I didn't know her name.
We had met before at her freshman orientation meeting.
We would pass in the halls or sit in the library exchanging
glances, but that's all. It was all so juvenile, but intriguing,
nonetheless. Plus, I didn't want to violate her amateur status,
at least not yet! There would be more to this story as we shall
see later on. I was studying but not feeling it during third
year until one winter day old Dr. F., my freshman biology
prof, accosted me in a hallway and suggested we go to an
entomological conference together at U…n College. I was
stunned. Stunned that he remembered me. Stunned that
he remembered that I had a passionate interest in all things
buggy; and stunned that he also invited my then girlfriend.
It all happened so fast. It was December when he picked us
up in his '70s VW Microbus and whisked us away to another
college town for the meeting. I was actually excited for a
change. The speaker was none other than Dr. Thomas Eisner,
the world renowned entomologist who spoke eloquently that
evening about the bombardier beetle. The talk was great,
the company even better. Dr. Eisner even shook my hand at
the end of the talk! Dr. F. dropped my girlfriend and I off

at our respective apartments. I remember starting sporadic visits to Dr. F.'s messy office and speaking with him about his extensive insect and coke bottle collection (he drank lots of Coca Cola). He specialized in fulgorid insects and related to me in no uncertain terms that he was a frustrated entomologist out of Cornell that could only secure a tenured professorship at a lowly pharmacy college teaching biology instead of entomology. I, too, was frustrated. He knew I loved entomology as well, and we bonded, sort of. He was still a spaced-out and weird character but I repeatedly thanked him for including me in that meeting with Dr. Eisner. He just smiled as he slurped down another Coke. My year magically started to improve in drips and drabs after that conference. Maybe that insect meeting jump-started something in me. My health slowly improved. My old flame and I fizzled out and I went back to an older sparkler, and then to a brand new spitfire. I just wanted a decent, blonde, hot girlfriend, one that put out. That's all. But didn't most guys on the planet? However, the best was yet to come, eventually. Dr. F. was a lousy Botany/Zoology professor but now I understood why; he was a bedeviled entomologist stuck in a pharmacy college teaching biological principles to mostly uncaring and cocky freshmen. I finally understood his conundrum, his mental state, and, perhaps my own.

54

Latin Scholar?

Are you kidding me? Now we had to learn Latin, as well? I had heard about this hokum from upperclassmen and figured if those knuckleheads could learn it, so could I. Actual pharmacy courses started third year. If you had achieved at least a C average through the first two liberal arts years, the college kept you for the duration of the pharmacy program. That was one sweet deal. So, third year Pharmacy I started and bingo, we had to immediately study that *dead* language. All doctors, including dentists, wrote prescription directives in Latin abbreviations, presumably to prevent patients from comprehending or forging them. That was probably the ancient and antiquated reason behind the formal and "secretive" transfer of information between doctor and pharmacist. But I believe modern medicine purposely perpetuated this sham past its prime. It became just one more egotistical weapon in doctors' arsenals of arrogance; patients were forging controlled substance scripts anyway. Nevertheless, back in my day pharmacists had to know how to READ prescriptions in order to fill and compound them accurately. The drug name was written in English, the rest in Latin. We students actually had exams testing our abilities to decipher and understand the often messy and awful scribbling found on most prescriptions at the time. By chance there was only a finite amount of Latin that was cogent to us plebes. However, this tepid foray into a foreign language was reverently considered a cornerstone of pharmacy practice. Much praise was heaped upon the wunderkind student that could correctly interpret an obscure and illegibly written Latin phrase on a prescription. Contrast that with today's computer sending of legible prescriptions to pharmacies to avoid confusion and mistakes. Glory be! Latin abbreviations are still used but at least they are clearly typed and identifiable. 1 TAB PO TID & HS UT DICT SECUNDUM ARTEM, baby! No more deceit.

55

The "Hated" Transfers

HATE is such a strong word, but if the shoe fits… One
third of our class was wiped out after second year; some
pharmacy students left for personal reasons, some for lack of
gray matter. That tuition drain had to be replaced, pronto.
Enter the dreaded transfer students. Although a few trickled
in before second year, third year saw the biggest influx.
That's when the real pharmacy courses started. We didn't
like them, we despised them, we were jealous of them.
They were brighter, better looking and more determined
than we "originals." Well, maybe not better looking. And
their arrogance and ambivalence toward we "originals,"
who had paid our dues with shitty first and second year
professors, only added to our disdain and hatred of them.
They formed their own cliques and had the temerity to
ostracize us; they had some gall! To be fair, they must have
looked upon us as Neanderthals, subhumans that resembled
"Old World Monkeys;" the indigenous species. They were
the improved "New World Monkeys," with better genetics.

Or were they? They came from other colleges and had to have an A average to successfully transfer in. Of course they were smarter than us. They had to be in order to get the limited transfer seats available. Some were much older than us; some even had prior careers. We hated "them." We felt they were just interlopers looking for a degree. WE had suffered real brain damage due to educational hardships and felt entitled to some homage. None was ever given to us. There was, however, some dating between our two groups. Sex is blind, after all. My former best friend F. started up with a transfer female; they are still married to this day. I guess it worked out for them. You never know. Our class valedictorian was a damn transfer; the Rho Chi Pharmacy College Honor Society was packed with them. I was not a member; there was no room for me. The ongoing animosity grew to such an extent that, at my wife's graduation ceremony, special "five-year" plaques were conspicuously alluded to and distributed to the "original" five-year plan students. Transfers were snubbed and subtly ridiculed. That's how bad things had gotten. I don't know how transfers are treated nowadays. In today's new climate of selfies and self-absorbed narcissism, perhaps no one really cares. I had tons of friends during my pharmacy college tenure and not one of them was a *dirty* transfer. Was I a bigoted and envious snob? You betcha. At my wife's and my separate class reunions, the "originals" and transfers could still be seen huddled in segregated groups; I guess our immaturity and long standing grudges still stood; almost forty years later, and counting. HATE is so hard to undo. Such monkeyshines from so-called adults, huh?

56

A Fly in the Ointment

Yes, it is a common saying. And yes, it literally did happen to me; I had documented witnesses. But first let's go back a few steps and review the Pharmacy I course and curriculum. Pharmacy I was our initial introduction to the world of pharmaceutical sciences. There was much to learn, memorize and make. It was taught by a seemingly stoic and dowdy looking middle-aged professor who was really a wild and crazy guy (ala Steve Martin) inside. You could just feel it. He was more than the nerd he projected professionally. Although at times hampered by a mild speech impediment ("sweet orange peel tincture" sounded more like sweet "oinge pee tinkcha" and "even though" became "eebbee dough") his classroom theatrics and feeble attempts at humor were appreciated. He did make a stupendous effort to get that "spiced" and torpid material across to us, though. And there were volumes of it, seriously. Firstly, we had to learn how to calculate. Yes, calculate. The initial course segment was called Pharm Calc. It involved mathematically deducing correct answers from "all sorts of problems" dealing with the conversions of percentages, weights and volumes of liquids, powders and solids. The exam questions were often convoluted, purposely confusing and sought to challenge the students' gray and white matters. A typical question was: A veterinarian seeks to have you make a 10% sulfur/aquaphor poultice for a 100g of product. If you only have a pre-existing quart bottle of 5% sulfur solution W/V., how many milliliters of said solution must be used to make the poultice? Calculating the ratios between dissimilar physical substances involved using our previous knowledge of chemistry, as well as fundamental math. It was not fun; it just made me mental. And since pharmacy in those days also vacillated between metric units and the old-fashioned avoirdupois (pounds) system, we had to learn how to use both measurements and to convert them as necessary. Another typical question was: How many drams (not grams) of a 3% hydrogen peroxide elixir V/V would be required to make a 41% standard gallon of product if 100 scruples of 4% peroxide W/W powder was previously added to it the day before? And we thought calculus was hard. Ha, ha. And besides learning how to calculate those endless cockamamie problems we were also quickly introduced to spirits, tinctures, powders, elixirs, lotions, potions, mouthwashes, ointments, creams, humectants, suppositories, etc. The list was exhaustive. We students had to mentally, and sometimes

physically, regurgitate all of these agents and their properties
on very difficult exams; and then use our "math" skills
to figure things out. We had to KNOW EVERYTHING
about pharmacy in a goddamn hurry! At least it seemed that
way. To do well on any given exam it paid to internalize
everything, especially the minutia. Prof H… had a sadistic
hankering for asking us the most obscure facts about
any given compound or confection. It became Wilson's
Law, named after one of our fellow classmates. He coined
the phrase, "Study the important things, then memorize
everything else." How true. Old exams were useless,
except maybe as guides for the misguided. The laboratory
sessions were basically exercises in accurate reproductions
of pharmaceutical products. Kind of like a cooking class,
following precise recipes and then being graded on the
final dish. Of course calculations were involved, to figure
out the exact amounts of ingredients needed and how to
prepare them before starting to mix, mold, kneed, triturate
and levigate. Alhough mostly obsolete in today's chain
drugstores, compounded medicines are still made in special
"compounding pharmacies" around the country. These select
pharmacies obviously must be profitable enough to keep
preparing some of those oldies but goodies from yesteryear.
And there are doctors still alive that keep ordering such
"forgotten" formulations. Go figure. Anyhow, we had a
large "Compounding" lab manual to follow, with a whole

year's worth of formulas inside, one for each three-hour lab period. The smart student would bone up on the upcoming labs and be prepared to *hit it* upon entering the large laboratory. Unprepared or lazy students would suffer, crib off of others or hand in sub par pieces of work. Although perhaps excessive and over the top at times, this lab did help prepare us to become REAL pharmacists, some day. We men also had to wear shirts, ties, dress slacks and a short, crisp white lab coat; women wore dresses and closed toed-shoes. Utmost professionalism was strictly enforced, this was a five-star culinary laboratory, dammit! All final hand-manufactured goods were labeled and handed in, to be graded on content and neatness. Levigation is a pharmacy technique used for incorporating a specific ingredient into a cream or ointment base and then spatulating it, with a thin-bladed metal spatula, in a certain back and forth motion to evenly disperse the ingredient in that base. One day, late in the year, lab time was running out and I was still furiously levigating a very sloppy and grimy Coal Tar Ointment when a housefly landed on my mixing pad, took a lick of the concoction, and promptly keeled over. I stopped working as did my two adjacent row mates. We had all seen what happened but couldn't quite believe it. After our excitement subsided, that feisty, fun-loving female, A. N., shouted from across the room, "Knowing that jokester Putz, he put that dead fly there himself." Well, I loudly protested

my innocence and lo and behold Mrs. B., a pharmacist and
lab instructor, came to my rescue. She saw the whole thing
go down and even signed off on my unfinished product,
that a fly had ruined it! I received an A that day, the fly
expired, and I just added another timely fiasco to my already
lengthy resume of comedic horseplay. I loved it. I also
remember Prof. H. running over to witness the commotion,
and then walking away shaking his head and muttering, "It
could only have happened to Putz, who else?" By the way,
Coal Tar prescription materials were used in those days
to treat psoriasis and other inflammatory skin problems.
Stinky, messy and toxic, it was a lethal mixture for dermatic
conditions and insects, as well.

57

Fortuitous Party

This is how all the *dental* madness actually started. It
was another rather innocuous but well attended third-
year pharmacy school party at D.'s apartment; you know,
the chap I was working with at the VA hospital. All
the regulars were already there. Even some girls showed
up. After I arrived, things really HEATED up. I had a
certain reputation in school. Fellow students didn't call
me the Smallman for nothing. Suddenly there was smoke
everywhere; it smelled like burned hemp. You know what
I mean. Pharmacy students really knew how to BLOW off
steam. Toward midnight, after numerous shenanigans, like
throwing a TV set out of a window, I chanced to bump
into a former well-known student who had graduated that
year. What he was doing at this soiree I'll never know.
Anyway, we spoke briefly during our encounter. "What are
you doing now, working for the family pharmacy business?,"
I yelled above the din. "No," he replied, "I'm a freshman
in dental school." I asked, "Dental school, where?" He

mumbled the location, it rhymed with Howard, but I didn't quite catch it. That was it. Thirty seconds of chit chat that changed my life forever. I just didn't realize it at the time. A dentist. All the noise, debauchery and bullshit at that party seemed to fade in an instant. A dentist. This guy had made it to the next level. If he could do it, why not me? I stumbled home shortly thereafter in a smoky and drunken daze but that dental thought was already firmly implanted deep in my skull. A dentist. Good grief!

58

P. Chem

I was a complete and certifiable idiot, although it seemed
like a good plan at the time. I had come off a good second
year academically, scored a solid A in Organic Chemistry
and felt cocky enough to think I knew chemistry. What an
imbecile I was. I didn't know chemistry. Inorganic Chem
had flummoxed me freshman year; Organic Chem was
merely an exercise in memorization. What a moron I was.
There were twenty-five really studious students signed up for
Physical Chemistry, the brightest bulbs in the class, and me.
I had a chance to take other electives such as The Novel or
World Religions, but no, my ego wanted validation that I
was a scientist and knew my chemistry. It turned into two
very painful semesters of humility. P. Chem was basically
a conglomeration of chemistry, calculus and physics, and
arguably recognized as the most difficult course in the
school. You had to have enough brains to reason out tough
problems and calculate your way out of extremely confusing
exams. It was taught by the "bad dream" tandem of the

Inorganic and Organic Chem profs. Although my frail condition during third year didn't help, I thought I could pull off this rigorous course. Besides, my new roommate was also in it. He was a very smart fellow who took great pride in never having to study. And I really mean that. I was there. I saw him NOT study. He was just TOO busy working his part-time pharmacy job and chasing good looking women. He was TOO good for college; it was just a means to an end. He never partied. He was in pharmacy college to get a job, get a wife and move on with life, as quickly as possible. His bloated ego assured me that together we would pull through. That sounded good to me. I studied, I panicked, I took chemistry advice from my roomie and still only managed a C- at midyear. My roommate was breezing through and managed an easy C, but he didn't care. It wasn't bad considering that he never took the plastic cover off the textbook and "lost" his lab manual. All this anguish was going on while I was laboring in other mentally strenuous courses like Pharmacy 1, Anatomy and Physiology, and Biochemistry. All four of those meaty subjects also had laborious laboratory sections as well. To compound my aggravation was the knowledge that some of my pals were taking the easy electives I previously mentioned and padding their GPAs with A's instead of C's. My wife still reminds me to this day that she got an A in The Novel during her third year while I received a C- in my damn elective. I was an arrogant dope; there, I said it. Anyway, at least the lab portion provided some levity for me. It was mostly unsupervised and held in the "special" P. Chem laboratory; basically a small, dimly lit room, shared with two professors' offices and a few makeshift tables stacked with all the requisite beakers, Bunsen burners, mixers, and glassware. Lining the lab were jugs and jugs of solid and liquid chemicals, some that should have been left alone by us. There were no laminar flow hoods, no ventilation access areas, just we hapless "chemists" using Worm Wood Oil, Chloroform, Toluene, Benzene, etc., toiling away in a small room with a locked window. I initially felt bad for the two professors who had to inhale the volatile and toxic fumes all day from our once weekly renegade experiments, until I found out who they were. One was that damned freshman English professor and the other, the ineffectual and derelict humanities instructor. Good, I hoped they inhaled deeply on our lab days. The labs were thankfully on the easy side and gave me ample time to experiment with various glassware; and the Smallbag was born. My devilish and probably misplaced ingenuity created a virtual smorgasbord of "glass" pieces that could be shaped into a multitude of configurations to toke out of. And a quick disassembly restored the benign objects back to form. Okay, so I stole some Ehrlenmyer flasks, rubber stoppers, corks, etc. from that lab. I admit it. My fellow P. Chem students all knew about my Smallman alter ego and "looked the other way" as I creatively pursued my "work." I would sometimes leave the lab to go into the hallway for a breath of real air. And on a few of those quick excursions I ran into (literally) my future girlfriend and wife, who, along with other freshmen, would be checking her answers against Inorganic Chemistry tests that were posted outside the P. Chem lab. I remember teasing her a few times, flustering her with my bluster, and thinking to myself how well she looked, but still could not recall her name. I believe the biggest windfall of P. Chem was not the learning of dubious chemistry, or my inventive collection of lab implements, but my discovery of batches and bundles of old Biochemistry exams in the tiny attic nook above the lab room. We students had noticed it from day one and my roomie and I finally climbed the steep ladder up into the forbidden zone. There was a sign that read The Forbidden Zone-Students Keep Out. Yeah, right. We had a lookout planted for us as we quickly rummaged around and then– SCORE, a treasure trove of tests, with answers! We descended the ladder with armloads of old Biochemistry exams. And it was funny how the smartest kids in that lab literally tackled me for a few copies. And those were the ones that were already pulling A's in that class. My own current, on again, off again smarty girlfriend was one of those that flattened me against the hardwood floor. And it wasn't out of love, either. Fortunately, my roomie and I saved some copies for ourselves. The biochemistry prof had a long standing habit of reusing a multitude of old test questions on his examinations. And boy did those old exams come in handy. I think I raised my average by a full grade because of them. That's how ridiculously hard Biochem was at the time. Unluckily for my future wife, that all changed when SHE made it to third year. That same Biochemistry prof had designed all new questions and her class got screwed. But for we deadbeats those were bonanza days and we benefited greatly. Well, Physical Chemistry finally came to a grinding halt at finals week and I eked out a C-, the lowest grade in that class. The laboratory portion had bailed me out but I was cowed nonetheless. My apartment mate got his gentlemen's C and was delighted. Anyhow, the agonizing yearlong chemical nightmare was mercifully over. What a waste of the few brain cells I still had left. My roommate eventually found his P. Chem lab manual under his car seat. It was still in mint condition. I "hated" smart students.

59

The Smallbag

What would the Smallman be without his Smallbag? Kind of like Felix the Cat without his Magic Bag; or a doctor without his steadfast and trusty black bag companion. Well, now I had a partner that made visits to parties along with me. This started during the latter half of third year and continued until graduation. It was a party favor, a dumpy duffle bag full of fun. But what was in that small, worn and rumpled blue/gray gym bag anyway? Why, glassware of all shapes and sizes, round flasks with rubber stoppers, pipettes, beakers, pins, pieces of cork, matches and odds and ends. Fellow partiers already knew about my eccentric sides; this addition to my moniker fazed no one. "The Doctor is in the house" people would yell whenever the Smallman showed up. "Let's all *shrivel* up!" Arranging the many breakable and delicate parts and pieces into certain shapes, like balloon animals, created a panoply of innovative toking implements. Why patronize a seedy Head shop when the Smallman could make something for you to indulge from free of charge? But of course it was temporary and was disassembled and cleaned after use, until the next party. The third-year Physical Chemistry laboratory unwittingly supplied the smoking instruments. The Smallman supplied his magical building skills and the rest was a hemp-stanking party! Nobody complained, nobody tattled. Those were HIGH times at pharmacy college. Of course we were the minority. The majority of pharmacy students were uptight and solidly virtuous, which is how it should have been. Most didn't dance, drink, smoke, nor chew. Wow. Sadly, the Smallbag was eventually retired, then abandoned, then pilfered. My future fiancée, then wife, had stowed it away rather casually in the cellar of her apartment house when I departed for dental school after I graduated. On a subsequent routine monthly booty call, I inquired about it and she found it and unzipped the rusty zipper. It was empty inside and my heart sank. All those memories, up in smoke. But then I remembered the secret compartment, unlocked it, and smiled, with a tear in my eye. There was the Smallman's pride and joy, a tiny but fully functional opal hash pipe, with the tarred screen still in place, inside the bowl. And next to it lay two small aluminum foil wrapped cubes. Come to papa!

60

The Halfway Party

Hooray, I sarcastically said out loud to myself, sounding more like Eeyore than the Smallman. Our tortuous pharmaceutical journey (aka pharmacy college) was officially half way over and done with. To celebrate this momentous milestone, our "warmhearted" college sprung for the elaborate annual party honoring we third-year *schlubs*. It was held at a ritzy, German-themed inn, a short drive from our campus. It was a dress-up formal affair, with mandatory dresses for the ladies and zoot suits for we *gentlemen*. Being a five-year program, the party was held at the halfway mark, in late January during the middle of our third year. It made sense. Some students were excited to check off this college bucket list occasion, this rite of passage; kind of like the prom in high school. I was lukewarm toward it, at best. I was still feeling funky and low, and not really in the mood for this kind of manufactured gaiety. However, there would be an open bar, authentic Deutsche bier and all you can eat sauerkraut, all night long. Ja sehr gut! As I polished my wing tips and aired out my moth ball infused suit, I couldn't help but reflect on the irony of the party's title and my fucked up lovelife, thus far. Was it a metaphor or a euphemism? A metaphor, I believe. The word "halfway" aptly and pathetically described my relationships with most of my paramours. Literally just prior to that big party, I had ditched a girl I had met a few months prior at Roscoe's. She was not one of us, having already graduated from a local state university. Plus, she already had a full-time job and a blue Ford Capri hatchback. She was a hotsy-totsy, buxom, green eyed, redhead and too much for me. Not physically but emotionally and psychologically. She saw marriage in our immediate future; I did not. I hated to part with her but I HAD to. It was too much. So, I asked the old original girlfriend, from freshman year, to accompany me. However, this time things were definitely ending between us, even the college rumor mill said so. We were already history, dead in the water, we just didn't know it yet. We ended up bumming a ride with two other couples in a cramped, egg-beater of a car. The trip started off with all passengers already in a dour mood and it went downhill from there. It degenerated into a road rage incident with our driver being sucker punched in the mouth. He had pulled over to discuss driving rules with a black-colored sedan when we were rushed by its occupants and attacked. Our pharmacy compatriot was slugged in the mouth through the open driver's side window and then he gunned it. We wimps were not prepared to fight. Plus, some of us were also wearing glasses. Our beaten driver ended up nursing a swollen jaw all evening and applying bags of ice to it instead of dancing with his girlfriend. It sucked for him, but she danced. The evening was quickly souring, despite the festive atmosphere and free drinks. And then I noticed some faculty members creeping out of the shadows from the deep recesses of the ballroom. Were they spying on us? Those sneaky little devils. Did we really need chaperons? Are you shittin' me? When the last tasty bratwursts and Lowenbrau pints were consumed, the party ended. It was midnight and time to head home. It had been a contrived party, but I didn't care. Hey, a party was a party and I was full of Spaten beer and wiener schnitzel. Prosit! The ride home was a sullen affair, however. My soon-to-be ex and I didn't even hold hands in the back seat. I desperately needed to get out of the slump I was in. Too many events had seemed to be conspiring against me lately. Perhaps I was just paranoid? The Halfway Party ended; it had been a major downer for me. I wish third year had ended, as well. Little did I know that in a few short months I would meet and mate with my future wife. Who knew? Ain't life grand, and sometimes a pick-me-up?

61

Electives

Most of the elective courses offered at PP College of Pharmacy in the late '70s and early '80s were a joke; or were they? In addition to the strenuous science/pharmacy themed electives, we were also offered choices such as World Religions, The Novel, Sociology, Human Sexuality, and Pop Psychology. Maybe the administration wanted us to broaden our views and not turn into complete science nincompoops? Ha, ha. Too late. But how difficult could these off-the-wall classes really be? Come on. These powder-puff courses were "taught" mainly by one asshole and he adamantly subscribed to a common scholastic version of Murphy's Law. You know, the easier the subject matter, the harder it is to get a good grade in it. During the first two years of college my GPA struggled even though I took some of those namby-pamby elective courses. So I thought I would be a *smart* guy by taking Physical Chemistry as an elective my third year. Holy shit was it hard. I was an idiot, again. First I was bamboozled

185

by the "easy" crap taught by that crappy professor, then I was thoroughly bushwhacked by chemistry that was way over my head, and hair! I hated "electives," I couldn't find a happy medium. I still hate that word.

62

Frogs A Leapin'

We *affectionately* called him Chuck the Fuck, behind his
back of course. He was the exceedingly handsome "silver
fox" third-year Anatomy and Physiology head professor that
allegedly had a "thing" for pharmacy college ladies. It was
never proven, however. And maybe he got a bum rap because
he also taught Human Sexuality as a third-year elective
course. My bunch of pals and I never took that "joke" class
because we had heard it was basically a continuous and
titillating soft-core porn show, legitimately presented on
the large screen in our big lecture hall, room #302. I took
Physical Chemistry as an elective that year because I thought
I understood chemistry. Not. An easy A in Human Sexuality
would have been much better, since I already knew so much
about the subject matter. What a JERK I was! Nevertheless,
the hard Anatomy and Physiology laboratory was a non stop
animal testing center involving a rotation of reptiles and
amphibians. Physiological inquiry of "simple" aquatic animals
taught us like-minded bottom feeders about electrical

conduction of nerves, which organs did what and how, and related our findings to the human body. The lecture portion was no picnic, either. However, the assistant instructor was a doll and helped many of us understand the salient material in spite of the frequent tyrannical outbursts and profanity laced barrages by her boss. And she greatly helped us in the lab portion as well. Thank you, E.N. The early semester laboratory sessions consisted of evaluating nerve conduction in decapitated frogs; not toads, just frogs. Of course, some still jumped; that was the point. We progressed to turtles, observing their live beating hearts. All in the name of science. Other experiments too gruesome to discuss were performed throughout the year and we absorbed the knowledge like worn out sponges, slowly but surely. We were tested in the lecture portion by half-baked short-answer exam questions that Professor Chuck thought were "easy;" and he ALWAYS admonished our class for being so stupid. I once had a heated argument in his office about a few of those questions and he summarily dismissed me as a "disgruntled ingrate," but changed my grade upward, accordingly. I guess he was fair after all, though still a rotten bastard. The lab portion was graded by handing in individual lab reports of our findings. Most of my buddies and I did OK in the labs and actually learned something. It was good to learn something. Maybe not readily useful, but good, anyway.

63

Upgrading

Am I still bitter? Maybe, maybe not. I believe we all got
what we deserved in the end. Nevertheless, the in-between
time was emotionally unpleasant, at least for me. What
am I talking about? The systematic and willful deluge
of pharmacy women into the local medical school and
law school libraries in hot pursuit of men, in lieu of us
pharmacy school "loser males." I once tried to gain entry
into those nearby libraries to honestly study; no dice. No
medical or law school ID's, no admittance! It's funny
how any female pharmacy student that wished entry was
instantly and reverently allowed in, no questions asked.
Very interesting but not surprising. I quickly surmised that
overworked and studious medical and law students had their
sexual needs, also. What else is new? But it was revolting to
us pharmacy guys. What were we, chopped liver? Evidently,
yes. And it was so obvious, too. Some of our ladies were
indeed successful at landing "big fish;" however most were
just fucked over by those arrogant pricks. During the

middle of third year, my own longstanding and vacillating girlfriend decided to abdicate, upgrade, and left me for a law student. I hope she got what she wished for. I was mad and distraught at the time but got over it and eventually ended up with a hot blonde. I cold-called my girlfriend of yesteryear out of curiosity; she reacted nonchalantly and stated that she was very happy with her marriage and workplace situation. God bless her. She was always a smart lass. I told her what I was doing and casually alluded to my net worth as a successful dentist. She seemed nonplussed, and I let it go. She and a few other women like her from my pharmacy college had traded in beta males for alphas, or did they? It has been over thirty-seven years now and my ex is still married, and happy. Perhaps she made the right choices after all, as I did.

64

Clueless Cavaliers

This vignette could have easily been named: foosball folly.
It was the second semester of my third year and a random
Thursday night found us in the same smoke-filled, hazy
establishment called Roscoe's. B. was playing front and I was
playing back, our usual arrangement on the bar's Hurricane
foosball table. We had a winning streak going and had been
playing intently for at least an hour and had no desire to
lose and vamoose. Practice made perfect and I was getting
better and better at this game. Two females approached
the table because it was their turn to play the winners,
us. One was a blonde, the other Asian, maybe Japanese?
That's all I remembered of that encounter. We annihilated
them with a shutout and never looked up once the whole
time. We were a hot team that night and wanted to keep
playing and winning. So who were the real losers that fated
evening? B. and I were. My wife reminds me that she and
her best friend, Y., purposely wanted to play us that night
to break the ice and "meet" us. She had a freshman's crush

on me and her girlfriend thought B. was cute. B. and I were
such stupes, and clueless, besides. I was in a foul mood, in
between girlfriends, and B. couldn't be bothered at the time.
However, we could have been nicer to them, perhaps looked
up and acknowledged them. But no, we were hunched over
that damn table, pulling and pushing on those rods like it
was a life or death struggle. B. and Y. never did get together
but that beautiful blonde and I did. We're still married
and she still reminds me of that ineffectual evening when
something could have happened, but nothing did.

65

F.O. the Mole Party

Of course that "righteous" party was held at my good
friend D.'s huge second floor apartment during the later
stages of third year. And of course it was well attended
and hilarious. D. and I worked together part time at the
VA Hospital pharmacy that year and became close friends.
He was cool, smart, and a fellow partyer. We had become
quite wearisome of the nonsense offered in Biochemistry
lectures and labs by that over-the-top mad scientist-of-
a-professor resembling old Doc Brown from the film
Back to the Future. He taught at a Ph.D. level and only a
handful of students actually understood him and thrived
in that course. His Bell's Palsy induced lisp did not help in
comprehending him, either. He was too smart for we smart
alecks. We called him Millimole behind his back. A typical
test question would read like this: If you had a V/V sulfuric
acid solution with a pKa of 6.0 mixed with a 0.6 MOLAL
solution of hydrochloric acid, what would the ensuing
stomach acid pH be if you imbibed the liquid and now

wished to convert the stomach acid environment to a 0.6 MOLAR solution, if the resting stomach pH was 5.0? How much of the sulfuric/hydrochloric acid solution would you need to swallow per minute if it weighed 6000 millimoles in V/W% and not W/W%? WTF? I'm not exaggerating. That was the "usual" type of question within a question that we were asked on exams. And the weekly, three-hour long lab sessions were often exasperating experiments in futility. Bunsen burners were alight, toxic chemicals and often caustic solutions were spilled everywhere and frustrated students could be seen running around cribbing from each other. Most of us were agitated beyond belief. Thank goodness only the lab write-ups were graded, and of these, most of our class fudged, with help from upperclassmen and our own smarty-pants classmates. Yes, we had a few of those. The prof had no use for us. We were beneath him intellectually, way beneath him; he knew it and took sadistic pleasure in it. Or maybe he was just ignorant and absent-minded? Perhaps. It's funny how I had this same exact experience with Biochemistry in dental school years later: the same type of bewildered students and arrogantly detached instructors, and the same types of ridiculous test questions and expectations. What is it about Biochem? So it was time for a blow-out pharmacy party to settle our frayed nerves from Biochemistry and forget about millimole malarkey for a night. D. posted the party in large block letters on the chalkboard in room 302, as usual, about a week before. And you know who erased it with quick vigor and relish? Millimole, himself. He didn't know the party was in his honor! The rest of the story was familiar; a party with lots of people present, from all different years, male and female. Everyone that "counted" was there. You know what I mean. The Smallman and his Smallbag showed up and got his thanks from the third-year classmates present for distributing old Biochem exams he and his roommate had found in the Physical Chemistry Laboratory. They ended up proving invaluable for most of the class passing that darn course. Then the loud revelry, the drinking and *smoking* ensued… However, the real significance of this particular party was the ludicrous theme, and the naming of it for a certain professor. I don't think he ever found out about it, or cared much if he did. And you all know what the F.O. stood for, right? The O. stood for the word *off.* Figure it out.

66

Hottie Blondie!

It's as if we had always known each other and finally HAD to meet; the attraction was that strong. But why? I don't know. We were not set up by friends or family and we seemingly only had one thing in common: pharmacy college. There was no Tinder, Match.com or EHarmony back then, either. Sure we had passed by each other in the halls all year, and sure we glanced at each other during those passing moments. And we were both committed to other mates at the time, but still there was this connection, this illusory sexual tension between us. But why? Was it only lust, a crush, a passing fancy? I had been this blonde's group orientation leader her first day at pharmacy college, was casually impressed by her, but had quickly forgotten her name. But she remembered mine. I was a veteran third year student, she, a newbie freshman. I was 20, she was 18. Maybe it was an upperclassman-underclassman sort of thing? Well, this went on all year, snatches of looks in the library, light teasing of her next to the Physical Chemistry lab, where freshman Inorganic Chemistry test scores were hung up. I was fully invested, or so I thought, in a myriad of women that third year, but this one kept piquing my interest. I finally had my chance to "officially" meet and greet her. It was late in the year, about two weeks before final exams, April 27, to be exact. I was tired that night, as was she. I had recently parted ways with a girlfriend, as did she and her boyfriend. There was a big party scheduled in a large apartment near the school. Oh goody, another chance for the Smallman to get his ego stroked and to indulge in some party favors. But I really wasn't up to it, mentally or physically. I was tired that night, as was she. What the hell, let's party! I showed up; she showed up with her female best friend, Y. I didn't see them at first because I was quickly ushered into the kitchen area to make the usual rounds with the hoi poloi and connoisseurs in some hemp sampling. As the Smallman, I had a reputation to keep up. I didn't have the Smallbag with me; no worries, though. As I finally exited the *haze-filled* kitchen area, I was mobbed by underclassmen wishing to get into my good graces. Everyone knew me and wanted a piece of me. It was exciting but tiring. I was tired. I just wanted to go home. But then, there she was. Sitting alone on that beat up living room couch. In the dim and smoky lighting, I could tell she was different than from what I had remembered. I hadn't seen her in a while. Wait, didn't I play foosball against her recently at Roscoe's? Anyway, she had slowly changed during the course of a year. The size 0, fair haired, blue-eyed beauty had evolved into a stunning and svelte, hot babe. And I was not going to waste any more time as I made a beeline over to her in a Goddamn hurry! Holy crap, she was pretty. Not so fast, big boy, not so fast. Oh, no. Two well known and well meaning second year students intercepted me on my way to that fateful sofa and engaged me with a "special" blunt. After five minutes of useless *small* talk and *inhaling,* I rudely and brusquely excused myself and literally ran for that futon. As I glanced back, the two underclassmen nodded and understood why I left them in the lurch, between hits, no less. She was a *hottie,* and all alone. I came, I looked, I conquered. Well, it was not that easy, but almost. Her friend Y. had recently departed that couch to go home, leaving my muse all alone. But she saw me finally advancing toward her and sat still. I approached and then proceeded to kneel down in front of her because my right shoe was untied. We started talking immediately but after about fifteen minutes she asked me if I was proposing to her or not? I laughed. After I tied that darned shoe, I had forgotten to rise back up again. I was that smitten. Foreshadowing? And my fatigue miraculously abated, as did hers, it appeared. But she had made it easy. It turns out that she had been patiently waiting for me to make this move for a whole year, through

her interloping boyfriends and my girlfriends. She just
knew I would come around. And she was right. The rest
of the evening was amazing. We had so much in common
and our future plans were in sync. She had heard of my
seemingly "sordid" reputation; she didn't care and told me
about her own "homegrown" preparedness for college. My
kind of girl. Maybe the Smalllady someday? Her father was
a pharmacist in the rural Adirondacks and an alumnus
of our fine institution. She was smart, sassy, fun and hot,
but kind of unassuming and quiet. What more could I
ask for? My previous girlfriends paled in comparison. We
left that party together, went to Roscoe's for a while, and
then I walked her home, and stayed overnight. Luckily her
roommate had been absent that night. We talked on the
phone the next day, went to a few more parties together,
instantly became the school's "new" couple and studied for
our final exams. Word spread fast about the Smallman's
new squeeze. People she didn't know came up to her and
said hello, in reverence to me. All of a sudden, she was
talked about, pointed at, lauded. She took it all in stride,
and with much pride. We only had a few days of school
left. With her parents' old, blue, Plymouth Duster, I helped
move her into a new apartment for her second year right
after finals. She invited me over for an appreciation dinner.
Now, all of my other girlfriends could barely prepare mac
and cheese, this one had a five course spread going when I

arrived at her new pad. I questioned her sincerity but she insisted that she always cooked like that. I was hooked. She had appreciated my help with her move and reciprocated by helping me move into my new lodgings. Those mountain girls are something else. Per her acquiescence and approval, I had managed to violate all her sensibilities, and other things as well, you know… But she must have liked my act because two children and thirty-seven years later, we are still married; and she's still my hottie blondie!

67

Apartment 3E

It was a crucial move but I didn't know it at the time. This apartment would be my home for the last two college years and play a pivotal role in the resurrection of my enthusiasm and health. I would finally have a great senior roommate, finally finish the pharmacy program, and make resolute future plans with my hottie blondie. It wasn't all smooth sailing at the beginning and that trend also continued deep into fourth year. Just before Action Central disbanded after second year, the word quickly spread about our manly break-up in our gossipy school. I hooked up with a fellow student that seemed OK; he appeared mature and had a car. Ambivalently we lived together through third year and stomached P. Chem together, along with many anguishing girlfriends on both our parts, and we reluctantly decided to keep on cohabiting, although in a different, cheaper section of town. Just before third year ended, we did score big however; we had unwittingly found our life partners, but who knew at the time? As stated previously, that know-it-all lazy roommate of mine was brilliant; however, he never studied, it was beneath him. I swear I never witnessed him taking notes in any class but he never skipped a single lecture or laboratory session. He always had a girl, a job and a tiny, bronze-colored, standard drive, Chevy Chevette. At least I got free rides to classes every morning. Most of my close buddies found him overbearing and distasteful. Just sayin'. Some called him shameful names behind his back. Oh well, I couldn't control that. Anyhow, we found this large apartment building by accident during a drive-by. It was very close to the Knox-Blox (Knox Avenue, etc.), a crime ridden, hellhole section of blocks; buildings for the monetarily challenged. I called the "for rent" number and we ended up signing a lease with a tall, well spoken Indian doctor that always looked queasy, as if he had made a bad real estate investment. And I'm not sure if he was Hindu or Sikh. He didn't wear a turban, but his lovely physician-wife wore a colorful sari and had that damn red omnipresent dot in between her eyes. Never mind. We had our new, two-bedroom place for less money and it had a parking lot in front. Winning! It was also very close to the college (fifteen-minute walk), grocery store (Ghetto Chopper) and, most importantly, Roscoe's! The lease on 3E began in June. My roommate left for his summer internship back home and I was left alone. No homecoming for me. By working part time all of the previous third year at the very coveted local VA hospital pharmacy, I was assured of a summer internship there, with relatively high pay (for an intern). And D. and I would be hobnobbing with the same close group of whacked out pharmacist rejects and retarded technicians we had become accustomed to working with. But this time I would be working full time, every day, for three months straight. I would get my internship signed off on and then quit, like everyone else did. After helping her move, hottie blondie went home to the Adirondacks and her black bears, moose and coyotes. She would be working simultaneously in her father's (class of '61) pharmacy and his wine shop (separate businesses but both necessary evils), besides waitressing at a friend's lakefront inn. Meanwhile, it was going to be a lonely and sexless summer for me, darn it. I really needed a car. Well, at least I had Roscoe's nearby and I could play foosball against the townies and Bandanna Man. There were few other pharmacy students around in the summertime. Roscoe's became a townie bar for the summers. Consequently, and out of boredom, I became rather good at foosball, running roughshod over the unsuspecting locals. My parents and girlfriend did come to visit me and I did borrow my grandfather's green-colored '72 AMC Hornet to visit my girl in the north country once or twice. But otherwise I worked, I ate, painted shitty acrylic paintings out of boredom, went to a few paltry gatherings at D.'s house, played foosball almost nightly, played some tennis, hated the extremely sweltering summer, and looked forward to feeling up my newly beloved when school, and my fourth year, commenced in the fall. My slump seemed to be abating and my mojo was slowly returning. And those fanciful dental thoughts were still in my cranial cavity.

68

Working for the Feds

Wow, third year had finally ended. Can I have an Amen? My GPA was a mess, a big waste; at least I was feeling better, though. Honestly speaking, the school year part-time job had been a serious pain. Not really tiring, just mostly inconvenient; I did end up studying and sleeping a bit less, however. And it made me grow up a little, too. We still had our parties but somehow I wasn't always in the mood like I used to be. Anyhow, no more school– summertime and full-time work at the local Veterans Administration Hospital was about to start! This was the payoff for working part time: the first leg (three months) of a required six-month internship. Plus, I would earn a good coin. The part-time job had consisted largely of clerical work, filing, pulling patient records, typing labels, answering phones, and dispensing drugs to veterans onsite. Full-time work for interns got us away from the "secretarial" end. Our pharmaceutical duties now included filling mail order prescriptions, compounding ointments, lotions and salves, and acting in the roles of real pharmacists. Although computers were around, none were used in the pharmacy service. Veterans waiting for their medicine had to pick a number and wait for it to appear on a large electronic "Bingo Board" in the stark waiting room, before approaching the bullet-proof window and pressing a button ("buzzing in") for help. It was the dark ages, what can I say? All the pharmacy work was also accomplished by hand, in a labor intensive environment, standing all day, with no music. Just fill, fill, fill those bottles with pills! Ah, the staff, or maybe staph, should I say? They were infectious and funny, weird and kooky. D. and I fit right in. As part-timers, we didn't interact much with the pharmacists; as full-timers, we were thrust into the mayhem from day one. The pharmacists, some old and some young, all had a "story." The VA was usually not the first choice for a job, you know. The Chief and Assistant Chief were NON-alumni from our college. It wasn't their fault that they were transferred separately from inner city VA's to upstate, N.Y. The staff cynically "knew" that it was "politically" motivated. They were both black and outsiders, a double whammy among our all white, local yokel staff. Oh, there was some animosity. Yes, there was. One incident almost turned ugly. It seemed that a certain administration-suck-up-female-pharmacist, who did the Chief's bidding and virtually no work on the floor, was up for Pharmacist of the Year, and was much ballyhooed by the Chief. That didn't sit well with the rank and file. The first annual "Fast Freddy Award," a hastily made-up cardboard-and-glue job trophy, complete with ribbons and lace, was presented by the staff to F.H., the pharmacist that had filled the most prescriptions in a year, at exactly the same day and time as the Pharmacist of the Year award ceremony, taking place at the back of the pharmacy. No one showed up at the back except for the Chief, the Assistant Chief and the back-stabbing awardee. The Chief was furious when he heard about the cake, all the commotion and congratulatory speech making up front. Boy, "they" loved to fuck with him. It all blew over, eventually. And the two-faced bitch did get a promotion, after all. It was the VA way! We interns witnessed it all and kept quiet, like a dysfunctional family unit. D. and I were officially "VA Boys" now. It was a sacred society. Ironically, although there were "whistle blower" signs posted everywhere, no one stuck her/his neck out even if personally witnessing some deleterious event. It was the VA way. True whistle blowers were punished, not rewarded. It was the VA way. The old-timer pharmacists warned us about the "VA way" and were all rather friendly. H.S. was in his late '60s. He didn't produce a lot but always had a spring in his step and made us smile whenever he uttered his catch phrase "Take a break." My young preceptor (the pharmacist who oversaw your work and signed the internship completion papers) probably suffered from PTSD because of the Vietnam War. Everyone called him Snarl, but I liked him. He was always good to me and taught me a lot about hospital pharmacy. He was fair-minded, a stickler for perfection and had a wicked sense of humor. He just didn't like being crossed or passed over for obvious promotions; that made him go ballistic! But the Chief loved to fuck with him, just to watch Snarl get his dander up. One time I gave a volunteer talk to the DENTAL service next door about non steroidal anti-inflammatories (Advil, etc.). It went OK. Little did I know that six years hence I would once again be a green tunic clad "VA Boy," this time in a distant inner city VA, in a very prestigious three-year DENTAL residency program. Foreshadowing is a bitch, and a joy? The summer was rushing by and I finally decided that I needed a vehicle. I was tired of bumming rides from D. and his old Dodge Swinger or continually hoofing it all over town. It was time for a ride of my own. I could then have the freedom to visit my girlfriend and parents, in that order. I heard Snarl wanted to get rid of his old college car. Maybe I would ask him. And that cute, smallish girl that had applied for a secretarial position way back when D. and I applied? She got the job also. And D. never went out with her, much to her chagrin. I had my steady up north and D. very quietly began dating another attractive secretary from our service. Only I knew they were going out together. They are still married to this day. The summer ended, D. and I received our signed "internship papers," and we were called in to see the Chief to get our "discharge papers." We would not be working during our fourth year and were done with the VA pharmacy service. Again, the Chief was cordial and sincere. D. and I had had a fun, joke-filled and party strewn summer; coming in late on occasion, sometimes hungover, sometimes spaced out and sick. It was all part of our lives back then. I asked the Chief for one more favor: hire my girlfriend as a part-timer, then intern, when she got to third year. He made me write her name down. That was it. D. and I left. And the Chief came through for hottie blondie a few years later. I had never fucked with him and he must have appreciated it. What a guy. A belated thank you C.D.

69

The Hemlock Hills Toucher

I already alluded to the fact that the summer after my third year was hellishly hot. I was working at the VA Hospital Pharmacy full time, fulfilling part of my internship requirement. The VA was in walking distance from my building complex and apt. 3E. The job was alright but the surrounding area was somewhat disquieting and sketchy. Not in the daytime, but mostly early mornings and late evenings. That's when things really heated up and went down. I didn't know that most of the criminal element was crepuscular in nature. Go figure. During the hottest part of July, an alert went out on our local TV and radio stations about an evening crime spree so despicable that viewers and listeners had to close and bolt all their windows and doors at bedtime. First the heat wave, now the crime wave. What was next? It seemed that the Hemlock Hills Toucher (our geographic area was known as Hemlock Hills) liked to break into unlocked and unsecured windows and doors, touch sleeping people and then literally run away. Nothing was ever stolen as far as reported. This had been going on now for about three weeks. Most other fellow apartment dwellers and I did not have central air in those days, or even window air conditioners for that matter. We were all poor, and cheap fans just pushed the hot air around. We were used to the soothing evening and nighttime breezes to help keep us cool and sane. Now we had to lock up and nail everything tight because of this weirdo lurking about our neighborhood. Everyone was hot and bothered, and steamed, besides. The temperatures and tempers climbed each evening in the ovens that doubled as apartment units. And he still managed to touch victims, darn it! My girlfriend came down from the chilly Adirondack hills that July to visit me and called me crazy for having my windows nailed shut and living in that overheated fire pit cube of an apartment. How could I stand the heat, she wailed? We were both uncomfortable and sweaty as we lay down to sleep. Sex was out of the question. She didn't visit me again. But the summer heat abated, the temperatures fell, and he vanished. He was never apprehended as the Hemlock Hills Toucher, although he may have been caught and prosecuted for something else, as is often the case. All "touching" had ceased before that autumn and I finally unnailed my shuttered windows. Nevertheless, the Toucher came and went but my girlfriend and I stayed together. The climate shifted in our favor that fall and we quickly rekindled our *hot* romance, if you know what I mean.

70

A Valiant Summer

The heat, the work, the loneliness. All were slowly taking
their toll on me that fateful summer after my third year,
while working at the local VA hospital pharmacy as an intern.
Maybe a car would help alleviate my doldrums. And then I
could readily visit my hottie blondie in the Adirondacks. But
where should I look? I had no money for a new auto; perhaps
a used one? I had enough dough for a really used one. I
looked through the local Sunday paper, asked some friends,
all to no avail. Kind of like suddenly deciding to start dating
and not knowing how or where to start! My preceptor, Snarl,
a VA pharmacist, came to my rescue, or did he? He had heard
that I wanted a used vehicle and matter-of-factly suggested I
purchase his old college car. At least now I had a solid lead.
He mentioned the price tag: 100 buckeroos. "That's all?" I
remarked. "That's enough!" chimed in a coworker and Snarl's
pal, V.R. I was puzzled but intrigued enough to check out
the car with Snarl during a break one day. It was a 1970 olive
green Plymouth Valiant. As I still saw plenty of them on the

roads, I figured they must be decent and reliable cars. I was
partly right. I couldn't quibble about the price; so what was
wrong with it? "Well," began Snarl, "It leaks oil badly, shakes
and shudders, is leaking radiator and transmission fluid,
and…" In other words, a junkyard would have had him pay
them to take it off his hands. I was crestfallen. But he was
still driving it to work every day. It was still functional, I
thought. Into the picture stepped my old man, the professor,
master builder and master at anything mechanical. If it
had parts and moved, he could fix it, period. My father and
his father drove over to my town, inspected the car, took it
for a test drive and declared it legally dead. However, the
price was right and I needed some wheels. I gave Snarl a
Benjamin and gave the keys to my pop. My grandfather
drove the family car home while following my father, later
sarcastically mentioning that he smelled burning engine oil
and could barely see through the black carburetor smoke
during the entire two-hour trip. A belated sorry shout out
to my deceased grandpa! My father knew that the slant-six
Chrysler engine in that Valiant was a great motor and was
confident that his automotive tinkering could restore the
car to brand new status. Of course, after spending a grand
and most of the summer on this project, which included
more than engine work, the car indeed was resurrected from
the scrap heap. I received it at home, a shimmering piece of
green metal that ran like a top. My dad was proud, I was

grateful, my girlfriend was ready for a visit, etc. I never paid
my father back the thousand he had spent on parts alone.
Thanks dad. I had to have it inspected and registered. I did
so in my hometown on a Monday morning and drove it back
to my college town, and to work. Snarl took one look at it
and grimaced. Why didn't HE have it repaired? Oh well, his
new car was a beauty, too. But I think he was secretly jealous.
This Valiant lasted me through the end of pharmacy college,
and through many trips, both summer and winter. The heater
didn't always work and the rear wheel drive made it slip and
slide in the snow. But it ALWAYS turned over and I drove
it hard; it was my trusty steed. I ended up "gifting" it to my
fiancée when I left for dental school. She loved the buttery
smooth power steering but froze inside in the wintertime. A
few years later, after an extended tune-up by the old man, my
new wife and I even drove it to Florida for our honeymoon.
Now, this car had been on life support for years, but it
still worked. We still used it well into the early '90s before
"gifting" it to my parents. My folks ended up having an extra
car to drive and they did so for a bunch of years more. It
finally broke down in the late '90s and had to be permanently
retired. All my father's miracle car fixing tricks had been
exhausted by then. It was finally and sadly junked. I still
remember all the fun times and accidents we had with it.
What a great car it was.

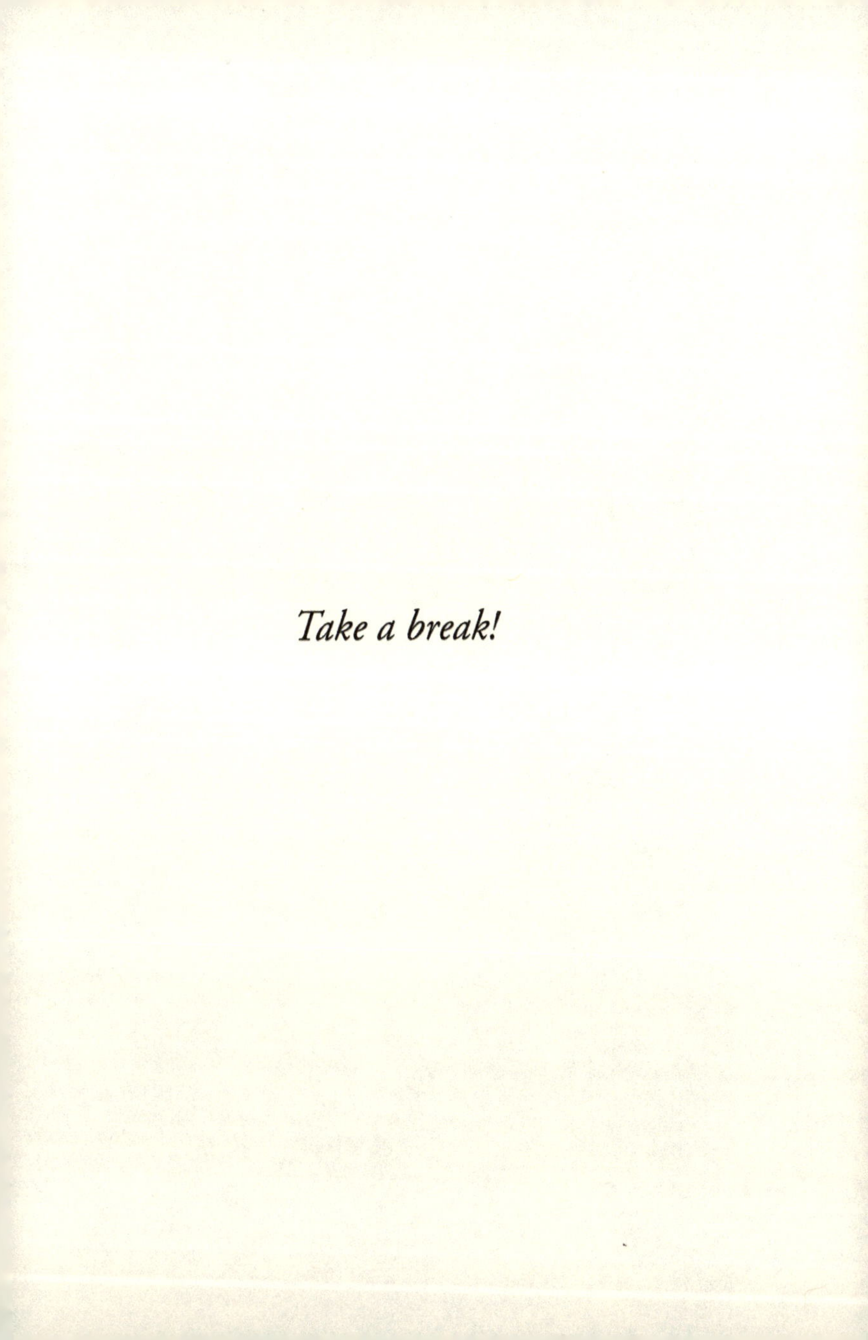

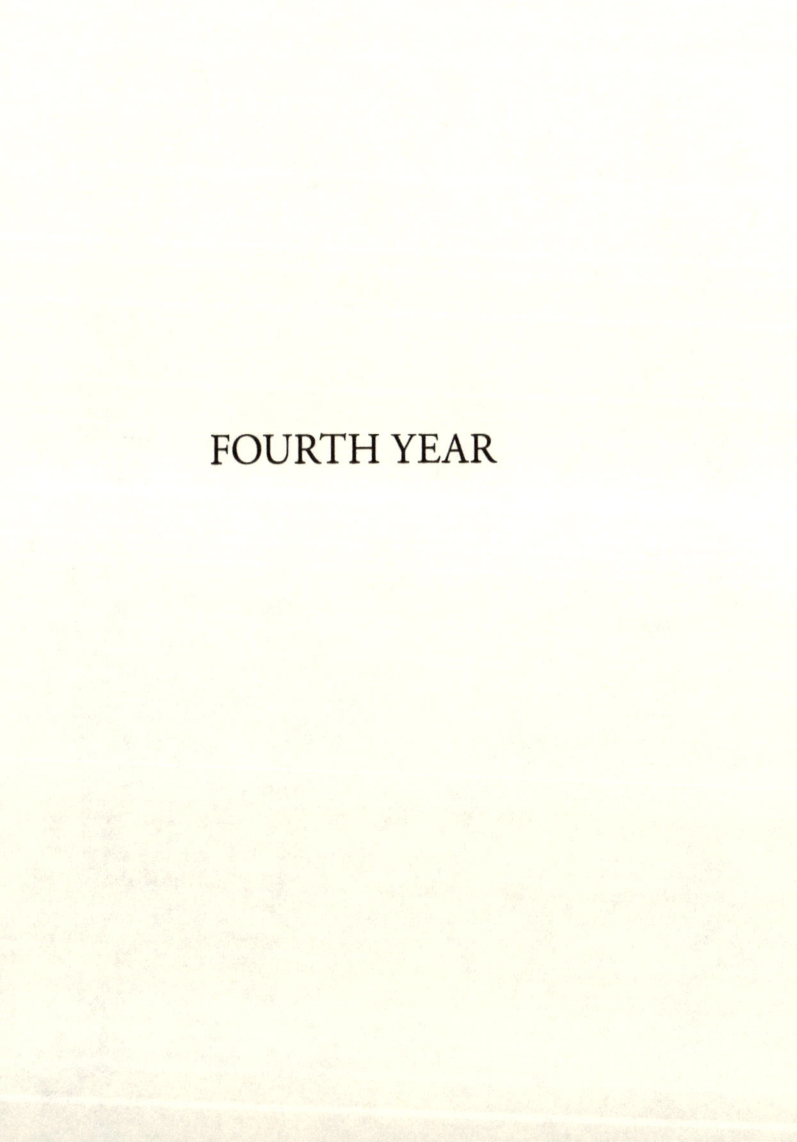

FOURTH YEAR

71

Med Tech Pricks

I was there, in the cafeteria, when those three prophetic words were loudly spoken at the beginning of fourth year by a slovenly attired and disheveled *study-wart* female transfer student: Med Tech Pricks. Was she referring to the small but legitimate group of "original" medical technology students that were to graduate in four years, unlike we pharmacy students in the five-year plan? Was she joshing? She had some nerve disrespecting them. Did she feel there was an unwritten pecking order in our pharmacy college: the "aboriginals," (us) followed by the transfers and then the "slime balls," the medical technology students? According to her sleep deprived and addled mind, yes. Are you kidding me? I can't believe what I heard. The Medical Technology game plan was a vibrant four-year B.S. degree program culminating in the dissemination of qualified medical technology personnel throughout our area hospitals. These students took the same courses as we did for the first two years of pharmacy college, then diverged into their own field of study. We had partied with them, respected them and bid them adieu, one year short of our own graduation as pharmacists. How dare a transfer student call them pricks? However, the name stuck and suddenly more students picked up that terrible moniker for those mostly female technologists. I sincerely hope they are no longer called that. Those pharmacy transfer students were nothing but trouble and a thorn in "our" backsides. Today, my alma mater boasts a myriad of degree programs, pharmacy being just one of them. I hope and pray that each student is respected and congratulated on her/his accomplishments and not vilified by some uppity, self-righteous transfer student!

Front Row vs. Back Row

It became obvious as our college's five-year plan dragged on. Sounds like the cumbersome Soviet Union five-year plans of yesteryear, doesn't it? Anyway, as we "matured" and became older and *wiser,* we *party animals* gradually ended up gravitating toward the back of every class and lecture hall during professorial presentations. The Smallman, his covert gang, and, a small contingent of other male "agnostics" and "naysayers," all took up residence in the last rows and seats available. It was a deliberate rebellious and nose-thumbing attitude toward authority. At least we felt that way at the time. We still listened, took notes, didn't fool around, and didn't talk, either. But we had that long-haired, *cool* and confident "thing" going on, both mentally and physically. And no "outlier" ever dared take our seats. The front rows consisted mainly of those fuckin' eager beavers, brown-nose twits, the beaming and winsome girls, the beta-males, the goody-two-shoes, kiss-ass types. You know who I mean. The professors would invariably engage the front row students in easy banter and with knowing looks; we just got the glares and the puzzled stares. And you know what happened at the end? Most of we "kill-joys" from the *back row* became super successful Ph.D.s, Pharm.D.s; and a dentist: me. Our front row brethren became mostly "normal," everyday pharmacy *schleppers.* I'm not sure what the psychological and sociological implications are here. I'm sure there were some. Later, as a dental student, I embodied the same principles of back row seating and not only graduated summa cum laude but landed a prestigious residency and, ultimately launched a most successful and lucrative career. To all students reading this vignette, don't be afraid of what others think; be yourselves, always. Was I really pompously and egotistically above the fray all those years ago? I don't know. But save a seat for me in the back row, please!

73

Dentures From Heaven?

It was embarrassing and quick. B. (aka the Foosball Wizard) and I were in a heated doubles foosball battle at Roscoe's that night. He was playing front, I was playing back, as usual. We were a decent team and played well together. It was crowded that late evening and pharmacy students were pushed up to the table. Oftentimes it was difficult to maneuver the rods because of someone's butt being in the way. When we played, we didn't drink. It was all business. However, the onlookers were usually blitzed by midnight, and this night was no exception. My good buddy was standing at my end of the table, sucking on a brewski with that drunk, shit-eating grin on his face. All of a sudden, something resembling teeth fell onto the table, right next to one of my men and the ball. And then, a hand came out of nowhere to snatch the object, and it disappeared, just as quickly. WTF? We all stopped play and looked up, around, and at each other in wonderment. What had just happened? It looked like teeth, falling from the ceiling, didn't it? I glanced over to my wasted pal, still standing there motionless and smiling as if nothing had happened. Then I remembered that he wore an upper denture. In his stuporous state, it must have slipped out of his mouth and unfortunately landed in the field of play. But he was still agile and quick enough to shove it back into his cake hole in the blink of an eye. Actually, it could have fallen on the dirty and disgusting floor and fractured. The foosball table broke its fall and saved his choppers! No one was the wiser and I didn't rat him out. A friend is a friend. I didn't tell B. about it because I'm sure he also knew. Ironically, nearly forty years after that incident, I'm still repairing, replacing and fabricating dentures as a dentist. Was that episode just a toothy snippet of foreshadowing? Perhaps.

74

Professional Practice

The title says it all. This particular class was a somewhat
enjoyable but demanding initiation into pharmacy as
a profession. A fourth-year course, it assumed that we
dummies had so far accumulated enough pharmaceutical,
medical and scientific knowledge to make it a logical
finishing class for budding young pharmacists. It was a
combination of classroom teaching about proprietary Over-
The-Counter (OTC) medicaments, such as dental products,
pain relievers and Band-Aids, and a "professional" laboratory
section relegated to compounding common prescription
medicines. Another very important piece of every lab session
consisted of being handed a pharmacy related item at the
beginning of the time period and then having to discuss
it with one of the professors in a consultative mode and
manner. These products could range from prescription
items to OTC agents. A student was often forced to not
only finish compounding the salve or ointment prescribed
but to also research and be prepared to be peppered with

questions about the prescription handed to her/him earlier. The mandatory student-made compounds were all shelved and graded by the staff. The consultative part was also graded. Each male student had to come to the laboratory in a crisp white shirt, conservative tie, polished dress shoes and sharp slacks. No bell bottoms were permitted. Women could not wear "hooker hose," short skirts, or open-toed shoes. Clean white lab tunics were also required. Professional attire, speech and deportment were the hallmarks of this course. The grading was stiff and exacting. No way could you bluff your way through this lab. Of course, one time I DID manage a perfect score for the laboratory period. I must have been sharp that day. We had to mix up a potion of psoriasis balm and dispense it in a one-ounce jar. I quickly and efficiently set up the ingredients, pestled them to death in a large ceramic mortar, added aquafor and stearic acid onto a large glass slab, and levigated the hell out of that concoction. My weight measurements had all been correct as I spooned the excrement-looking mixture into a one-ounce glass jar, affixed the necessary and appropriate prescription label onto its surface, and handed it in. Done with Part 1. Part 2 consisted of a female contraceptive device, called the Diaphragm, popular in those days. It was a female barrier device used in conjunction with contraceptive jelly for prevention of pregnancy. Remember, no deposit, no return. This was going to be a no-brainer. Ha! Hottie blondie used one exclusively. It was shaped like a circular, smooth, tan-colored turtle, minus the head, tail, and appendages. One of my body parts nudged that piece of convex rubber on a regular basis. I knew all about it, intimately. This was going to be an easy consultation. And, it was. The head professor, who had a habit of holding up his large right hand in front of his usually expressionless face as if giving us all the finger, looked surprised and astonished at my knowledge and forthright way of elaborating on such a touchy subject: female contraception. He actually congratulated me in his droll and understated way on my aplomb, after we had finished. I think I scored many Brownie points that day which helped me in my final grade for the course. Thank you, hottie blondie.

75

High Water Pants

Dr. Wally A. was our hopelessly out of touch professor of Biopharmaceutics and Pharmaco-kinetics, a fourth year bitch of a course and often shortened to just Pharm. II. He was fresh out of industry somewhere, and came in spouting off colloquial jargon that was over my head. He reveled in his superiority and gleefully confounded we students to no end. We were openly fed up with his "knowledgeable" diatribes and tangents during class. Shamefully and to his discredit, we often failed to grasp the basic tenets he tried to teach us. I agree it was a difficult course but he made it harder by being such a twerp. And his dated '70s attire didn't help his cause. Paisley shirts, ill-fitting suede jackets, platform disco shoes and colorful high water pants made him look like a poorly tricked out pimp wannabe, masquerading as a lecturer. A bad teacher, a bad dresser, and running a bad laboratory: a triple whammy for us. The course was designed for us to learn the mechanisms of how medicines reacted in the body, at what rate, what potency and what effectiveness, all based on the drug's formulation. As a professor, he failed; as a man, who the fuck knew? However, he probably liked women. How did I know? A certain raven-haired and *hot* female would always come to that class fashionably late, usually clad in black and without a bra on. N.P. liked to flaunt her bod and always wore hip-hugging yoga pants. She would always make him stand up and notice, which made his slacks ride up. He would chide her briefly but the bulge against his front zipper gave away his true feelings for her and made his pants rise even higher. Our "original" pharmacy sisters hated and shunned her. She was one of those damn transfer students and most likely perceived as a threat and cock-tease in their eyes. Women can be so harsh and judgmental on their own sex. We heard that she was dating a ski bum and chef from Upstate N.Y. and didn't have "time" for we adolescent minors. She was WAY too good for the ogling prof, too, I suspect. However, I also heard that she never graduated, having quit after the fourth year because she was too *cool* for all that pharmacy gibberish. I hope she is happy somewhere, skiing and still looking hot. But, probably not. Anyhow, the laboratory portion was a continuation of the Pharmacy I laboratory although a lot harder, with more advanced formulations and products to fabricate. We "graduated" to more hands-on product making such as hand-rolled suppositories, endless emulsions using the mortar and pestle, complicated ear and eye liquid agents that involved Bunsen burners, etc. Nevertheless, as a class, we were ready for that level of difficulty. We weighed, rolled, measured, mixed and boxed our products to be weighed, assayed and graded. That was going to be our lives, so we thought back then. Compounding pharmaceuticals was a chemically noble endeavor found only in the realm of pharmacy. And only pharmacists understood and could produce such mystifying medications from illegible and secretive prescriptions. We were on our way to be certified druggists. Yay. And Doctor Wally A.? He lasted a few years before rejoining industrial pharmacy from whence he had originally come. Good riddance, and good riddance to his shiny, gold-colored, disco shoes, as well!

76

Emotion Lotion

Well, Pharm. II lab was all drudgery with meticulous measurements and attention to detail. And student competency was constantly analyzed, recorded and reflected in our GPAs. I realized that the school was not so secretly preparing us for the pharmacy board exams, so we had to know our shit, cold. However once in a while, on a whim, we were permitted to indulge our pharmaceutical fantasies and whimsical sides and produce a legitimate concoction, but with an original flair. Kind of like making regular hamburgers but with soy sauce mixed in them. You know, still legit but a little different and unique. It was done to give students some creativity and a day off from the rigorous grading police. We still, however, had to wear professional duds in the lab. Anyhow, I knew just what to prepare. I had been dating hottie blondie for close to six months now and decided a thoughtful present was due her. I knew from personal observation that she loved to slather herself nightly with various store-bought lotions,

potions, ointments, pomades and creams, such as Aveeno
and Noxzema. So being a decent but financially strapped
boyfriend, I decided to fabricate her some "personal"
lotion from me. And it wouldn't cost me a dime. It was on
the school's nickel. Bonus. The lab atmosphere was relaxed
that day, with classmates busy making all kinds of weird
and stinky goods. We were finally having fun with no
pressure to excel. I mixed up a basic White Lotion, with
zinc sulfate, sulfurated potash and water as ingredients.
And instead of making a small 30-ounce amount, I made
nearly a pint. To this I added a tiny eutectic mix of
thymol and camphor to give the lotion some zing. Lastly, I
stirred in a small amount of artificial strawberry flavoring,
which gave it a rose-colored hue and sweet strawberry
odor. I labeled it "Emotion Lotion," to much ribbing
from the professors present. They knew it was for my
girlfriend and nodded their approval. R.W., my row mate
to my right, however, was busy rolling and shaping dozens
of cocoa butter suppositories with some dark, esoteric
ingredients added. I made a queasy quizzical face as I
looked over at him and asked, "Where are you going to
stick those black beauties?" He laughed sheepishly and said
they were for a gag gift. I wasn't so sure, knowing him.
Anyway, my girlfriend really appreciated my efforts and
loved her token of appreciation for putting up with me.
She added it to her armada of nightly beautifying agents

that women tended to use before bedtime. Many a night I would smell that wonderful aroma of strawberries on her face and think about our emotions for each other.

77

Buzzy

He was a punk-ass barn cat through and through
for goodness sake. He wasn't meant to live in a puny
apartment. But there he was, an orange and white striped,
un-neutered male kitten named Buzzy, ready to rumble!
My fourth-year roommate's girlfriend acquired him, quite
literally, from her family's barn and thought he would
make a cute and cuddly addition to we four humans
in 3E. Not! After repeatedly biting and scratching us,
buzzing around the rooms non stop, ripping up our
gossamer curtains and the underside of my bed, he was
hastily and apologetically returned. His name wasn't lost
on me, however. Many was the time when we were all
buzzed at the apartment, especially during my upcoming
fifth (senior) year. Anyhow, stinky litter and kitty food
notwithstanding, he was just not a good fit for living
peacefully with people who were gone most of the day.
Another feline might have worked but we didn't try
THAT experiment again. Being a cat lover myself, I

hope he lived a long and happy life chasing and catching rodents and vermin in that barn of his. Don't get a barn cat, even if it's for free.

78

Toxic Shock Syndrome

Although based in fact, this is not an amusing story.
However, it does showcase the humanity and concern of
a particular professor, whom I greatly admired. Dr. H.
was a tall, thin, gray-haired professor of microbiology and
immunology, consecutive fourth-year courses at PP College
of Pharmacy. His very deliberate and slow way of speaking
was sometimes annoying and disconcerting, but he always
got his points across clearly and concisely. I learned more
from those two courses than from many others put together.
He made the cause and effect ministrations of drugs on
pathological microbes, both bacteria and viruses, logical and
seamless. He was cutting edge in his information, and we
all benefited as future pharmacists. Nevertheless, his tests
were very difficult, but fair. They were all multiple-multiple
choice types of exams. Each question had many parts to
consider before answering it. You had to know your shit and
not get rattled! If you studied your notes carefully and had a
decent memory, paid attention in the classroom and the labs,

you would be rewarded. Before exams you could peer into
his lab and see him sitting alone with perfect posture, over
a manual typewriter, hacking away at the keys, typing out
brand new questions. He was no dummy. Old exams helped
in his courses, but you still had to study. There were few
repeat questions asked. Observing him in that darkened and
spooky lab was like watching an executioner from the Middle
Ages slowly sharpening his blade before the judgment day.
Even one of the outside laboratory doors had an archaic word
written on it: Bacteriology. That name obviously excluded
viruses, plasmodia and prions. It harkened back to when
our college was first constructed, the 1800s, when those life
forms were either not yet discovered, discussed or in vogue.
I wasn't surprised that the lab doors were still the originals,
and unaltered. Now, let's move ahead to our present time
period in the early 1980s, but still keeping on the subject of
microbiology. A new and improved super-absorbent tampon
became all the rage. It was called Rely. But, suddenly, reports
began circulating that it was causing toxic shock syndrome
and fatalities. Supposedly its success led to staph infections
in susceptible women, with dire consequences. Old Dr. H.
took it upon himself to educate the pharmacy college women
on the dangers of this feminine hygiene product. It was a big
deal for him to organize such an event, to purposely exclude
the men, and talk intimately and openly with the ladies about
such a delicate subject. However, he pulled it off after hours,

in our largest lecture hall, with much appreciation from the womenfolk. That's the kind of professor he was. Understated, kind, soft-spoken but smart and direct. He seemed to be lost in the deck however because other cocky professors thought they were "real" cards. They may have had more bluster, notoriety and bravado, but not brains. I liked Doctor H. and often interjected his namesake in a positive way during times when other instructors' names came up in derogatory diatribes, which was often. My buds would stare at me because I had nothing bad to comment about him. He was a great teacher and gentleman; what can I say?

79

Playing House

Did the "marriage dogma" start early for me? I believe it did. I know it did big time for my fourth-year apartment mate and his live-in lover. They played house for real, for close to a year, before moving on to their own private digs. Hottie blondie and I dabbled at pseudo-marriage that year, although we still had separate living quarters. I was in my fourth year and she in her second, at pharmacy college. We coexisted as best as we could in two different apartments with very different roommate personalities present. In my girlfriend's place, it was usually quiet and numbingly tense. Girls studying, no boyfriends, no makeup, no sex, no nothing. At MY apartment, rock music would be blaring and it wasn't unusual for that "live-in" gal to physically drag my apartment mate into their bedroom, only to emerge quite ruffled five minutes later and announce to us, "How do you like the 'just laid look'?" We laughed, knowingly. They were both horny bastards, too. But coupling WAS the norm at our college, especially between committed pharmacy students.

Studying and sex became our norm, also. But there was more. My girlfriend and I would regularly go food and clothes shopping together, did the laundry, paid the rent, utility and phone bills, etc. She did all of the cleaning and cooking while I supplied her with old exams, my notes and highlighted textbooks. My car was "our" car and she frequently drove it as needed. Were things fair between us? I don't know. We never really looked at it that way. We still had separate bank accounts in our parents' names, however, and only bought food jointly. And we went on walks to parks, took drives, and attended parties as a team; the lack of dorms made us grow up quickly. There was also plenty of cuddling but no coddling. We had gotten a lot of "couples' angst and jitters" out of the way by technically living together. This form of cohabitation, juggling living spaces and disparate roommates, with the same sexual paradigm, continued until my graduation the following year. I'm not saying our lifestyle was right or wrong. It worked for us at the time. And we were not that unique or unusual, except for our absurd frequency of intimacy, perhaps. That I knew for a fact. I recently heard that my former fourth-year roomie and his hot-and-bothered flame are now divorced. I'm not surprised at their flame-out. I'm still married to hottie blondie. You never know how things will heat up and turn out.

80

The Southern Comfort Affair

I'm almost embarrassed to admit it, but here goes. The Smallman and his lady were invited to D.'s house for a Hairy Buffalo party. Nothing unusual there. A Hairy Buffalo mixer involved the attendees to bring any kind of hooch and empty it into a large, presumably clean, plastic garbage barrel. To this alcoholic mixture was added fruit punch such as Hi-C, and voila, a Hairy Buffalo was born. It was a high proof and potent broth that would quickly make the unwary drunk in a hurry. But the *boyz* in that house cheated. Any good quality booze, beer or wine was quickly absconded to be used later by only them. Most of the revelers didn't know this, except for me, of course. My keen eye had picked up on this chicanery at previous parties held there. So, only cheap liquor ended up being dumped into that vat of nebulous brew, while being ceremoniously stirred by a "clean" baseball bat. I liked D., he was a good friend. We had worked together at the VA. However, I knew it was stupid to bring anything of quality to his apartment. It was already late that Friday night; hottie blondie and I were finished studying for the evening and got ready for the party. Oh, no; we were at her place and she anxiously informed me that all we had in her house was an inch of Southern Comfort whiskey. That was it. However, I wasn't about to drive to a liquor shop to buy a bottle of cheap spirits for that dang Hairy Buffalo. No way. So, we used our pharmaceutical skills and wits to improvise. Thinking fast, my girlfriend produced a bottle of Triaminic cough syrup from her bathroom. It matched the shade of the whiskey perfectly. We poured in the syrup to about the halfway mark and filled the rest with tap water and shook the contents. When all was settled, the Southern Comfort half-pint bottle looked authentic and even smelled of alcohol, but just barely. Confident of our ruse, we boldly entered D.'s domicile to join the fray. We were immediately accosted by his jocular roommate and handed a lit bong, shaped like a very old-fashioned telephone. My girlfriend and I were implored to "say hello" into the speaker portion and received a complimentary bong hit. It was corny but a riot. Most of the entrants were not given this treatment. Only a select few, including the Smallman and his significant other were extended this *stoner* courtesy. It was much appreciated, especially with envious partiers looking on. We were party royalty, what can I say? Hottie blondie and I entered the kitchen area and produced

our contributory bottle of fire water, whose contents were
to be added to the quarter-filled garbage can. But wait.
Another one of D.'s roommates quickly swooped down
off his perch on the counter and grabbed at the Southern
Comfort in my hand. He claimed he wanted a taste and
then wanted to pass it around. Yeah, right. I knew better.
I knew where it was going to go. Into his bedroom to be
drunk later. However, he made a scene, loudly protesting
that the Smallman would not give it up to a host. I didn't
care, ripped out the cork, and poured the doctored contents
into the bottomless garbage can, as he almost cried. I didn't
want to get caught with a Mickey Finn, plus fuck him.
He was an asshole anyway. People in the kitchen stared at
me but no one said a word. The Smallman had clout, you
know. Things simmered down after that and no one was the
wiser. My girlfriend and I had some of that rotgut punch
and quickly became smashed. Hopefully, our addition to
that conglomeration of alcohols prevented guests from
getting a cold. I mean, the added Triaminic was a potent
medicine, even though at a minuscule percentage. I believe
we did a "good deed" that night, although deviously.

81

Of Mice And Rats

No, I'm not talking about the two different types of professors at my pharmacy college, although perhaps I should. No, I'm speaking instead of the fourth-year Pharmacology laboratory periods where we lowly rodents experimented on real life, lowly rodents: mice and rats to be exact. Before we "graduated" to cats, we had to wade through a boatload of experiments involving little white mice and large albino rats. Most of the mouse experiments involved injecting dozens of them with calculated formulations of different drugs and then observing the effects. Of course the drug mixtures had to be prepared properly before needling the mice. After my pal and future roommate B. pulled taut the skin on their backs, I quickly injected the belly portions with the various drugs and then B. would place the drugged mice inside tiny cages. We seemed to be very adept at this kind of lab work. Some other classmates, not so much. Some were squeamish, some uncoordinated, and some were just plain puzzled at what to

do. During one of those laboratory sessions, A.N., a witty
and wise-cracking female classmate called out, "Hey, not
fair, those guys know how to play darts," while pointing an
accusatory middle finger at us. B., I, and our other three
lab mates chuckled as others stared at our proficiency with
the white vermin in front of us. Well, it's true that we
did play darts regularly but we didn't throw the syringed
needles at the rodents, we jabbed them at very short
distances. Give me a break! So, after a few minutes, the
various medication-addled mice started to exhibit specific
symptoms of drug effects which we had to dutifully record.
My favorite was the "wide awake drunk syndrome," caused
by the simultaneous administration of caffeine and alcohol.
The mouse was awake but stumbled all around the cage.
A very valuable lesson that caffeine does squat to sober
up an intoxicated individual. The rat labs were a *trip*. My
favorite was to administer morphine to a rat and then to
put a wooden clothespin on its hairless tail. It didn't feel a
thing because it was in la la land. Then we gave it a shot
of prepared Narcan, an opioid reversal agent, and timed
how long it took for the rat to feel the pinching of its tail.
If we had accurately mixed up the Narcan solution, our
timed experiment would be "correct;" if not, we failed. We
progressed to cats later in the year. I will discuss that in the
next vignette. Suffice it to say that all the experimentation
in that lab led to group presentations in front of the

Pharmacology professors at specially convened times. It was a rigorous testing of our knowledge and pharmacological acumen. Our particular group usually didn't fare too well because we were not suck-ups or brown noses. We knew our material but it didn't matter. We took our B's begrudgingly and moved on.

82

The Cat Bucket

As a cat lover what I am about to relate to you pains me, but it was a necessary learning tool in pharmacy college at the time. Fourth-year Pharmacology lab was a non stop animal testing ground involving all sorts of furry creatures; cats were on the lab slabs toward the end of the school year. The pharmacological inquiry of animals involved running drug-testing experiments on them. The ensuing results were basically extrapolated to the human body. It was a bit sadistic but commonplace in a scientific setting. As we matured as pharmacy students and "pseudo-scientists," the laboratory experiments became more difficult and involved. Intense attention to detail was required as well as scholarly note taking during the sessions because our findings were graded harshly later during the week. The lecture portion was no picnic either, with frequent unannounced quizzes from a pretentious and cranky professor, Dr. M., who delighted in torturing already miserable students by asking triple negative test questions on his major exams. However, this was the "heavy course" in pharmacy college, the one that we all needed to learn from: how drugs work in the body and what organ systems were affected. It was just a tough-ass class with a lab to match. Anyway, we progressed to cats. These felines were supposedly strays that had used up all nine of their respective lives in animal shelters. No one wanted them except our college. They did look sickly and mangy but it was hard to tell for sure. As we walked into the laboratory, each of the ten "stations" had an anesthetized cat lying on its side with electrical wires attached to it, both externally and internally. We usually worked in the same groups all year and five of us would approach the "business area" together and begin the experiments and observations required that day. We were asked to properly mix and administer various drug formulations to the said cat intravenously and then watch what happened. A detailed polygraph type readout would give us information about the organs tested, such as heart rate, respiration rate, bowel movements, etc. If our calculations of the drugs given were incorrect, we would all fail as a group. If we were correct in our pharmacy calibrations and started to get the desired results midway through the session, we could proceed. Those were anxious moments for already keyed up, nervous students. The two or three skulking lab instructors included the kindly and old, part-time pharmacologist Dr. S., who would walk around with a lit Camel cigarette behind his back and monitor our progress like a hawk; nothing was missed. You could hear a pin drop in the lab that always faintly stank of stale cigarette smoke. No one wanted to fail, so nary a word was aired about the forbidden smoking in the lab. There were "No Smoking Because Of Combustible Chemical Vapors" signs posted, but, whatever… None of us blew up. All the students were too busy furiously note taking and whispering among themselves to finalize a standardized version of events that transpired. Later in the week a scheduled private conference was held with five of us lab partners in attendance. If by chance you got the smoking Dr. S., who was notably hard of hearing, just by saying the word "creases" usually got you off the hook from a challenging question. You see, most of the questions required the student to reply "increases" or "decreases" as related to the experiments we employed. Not so with the head professor Dr. M. He was a bear, and kind of resembled one, and had his favored bunches of like-minded, highbrow students. My group was definitely not on that list. Those "other" groups with a mix of smart and dumb students often received A's as a team, if they were favorites of Dr. M. Our team kept getting murdered with B's, no matter what our answers were. It was nerve wracking, but what could we do? We were no dream team but, hey, we were not ignoramuses either. Those "retards" that pulled A's because of their intelligent group members really got us royally riled up, at times. Oh, well. Life isn't always fair.

Hats off to Dr. S. for at least making Pharmacology less intimidating and grading OUR group fairly. He gave us a few A's during the year, thanks to "creases!" What happened to the cats? They were dumped. How? Firstly, a lethal dose of potassium chloride was administered to humanely euthanize them, then we unceremoniously grabbed their tails and tossed them into a very large bucket labeled The Cat Bucket. When the profs weren't looking, some of my *sick* buds would throw their cats across the room to make a basket, so to speak. I don't know where the felines were ultimately disposed of. I wanted to make this a light-hearted read but could not. Those cats sacrificed their lives so I could learn how my liver and onions worked.

83

Cheese It, Here Comes the Dean

Our pharmacy college dean at the time was a height-
challenged but formidable pit bull. Seemingly placid and
non verbose, he was tough as nails if a situation warranted
it and a man not to be trifled with, EVER. Enough said.
Pharmacy college was supposed to be devoid of deviant
students taking pleasure from illegal drugs, period. However,
this was the very early '80s, that post '70s malcontent era
of remaining decadence and malaise. The last vestiges of
that "drug" period were ending fast, but not soon enough,
especially for our college administration types, including
the dean. I have already mentioned all the private and
sanctioned get-togethers that we pharmacy students had
willingly and wantonly participated in on a regular basis,
well, at least by the *cool* ones. And I have alluded to the
naked truth that many of those soirees were indeed laced
with a bit of dope, from time to time. Nancy Reagan had
said "Just Say No." I was fond of saying "Just Say Yes." One
of those parties got a surprise visitor one memorable night,

and it was not a Norman or Jehovah's Witness, either. It was the Old Man, the dean himself. Holy shit! The party on Delaware Avenue was well attended that evening. The Smallman, his Smallbag, and his hottie blondie were common fixtures at parties and this one was no exception. It was hosted by four classmates of mine that I didn't know very well. We kind of traveled in different circles, but I sporadically mingled with them and we had a modicum of respect for one another. They were Okay. B. was there, as were my pals P., D., and other letters of the party alphabet. Curiously though, Johnson and F., former Action Central alumni, were absent. But I wasn't surprised. They had veered off onto questionably boring and different paths years ago. But, to each his own. Anyhow, The Smallbag was unpacked and in full use by midnight. Most of the "kitchen brigade" had already passed around some bones numerous times. The hard rock music was blaring and most of us were feeling no pain, for the moment. Then the doorbell started buzzing and buzzing. Who the fuck could be trying to get into a party that was just about over? T.R., one of the hosts, angrily tore open the front door and then nearly fainted, so I heard. I was in the kitchen when I heard the whisper, "Cheese it, here comes the dean." We quickly stashed all our "stuff" into garbage containers and just sat there, ready for the inquisition. The music was instantly cut and windows surreptitiously cracked for ventilation. The dean, the assistant dean, and a few other PP College of Pharmacy officials confidently strode through the apartment, nodding but not saying a word. Was a search warrant warranted? Who knew the laws back then? The unwelcome bunch quickly showed their poker faces in the kitchen, turned around and stalked back into the living room. The dean finally spoke. He cleared his throat and in a gravelly voice said, "Keep the music down, boys. And, let's wrap it up." That was it, as he and his bootlickers left. I mean, he wasn't stupid. He knew what we were allegedly and illicitly up to; what we were toking, etc. He had a nose. But he chose the high road. I immediately gained the utmost respect for the guy. He could have canned us all, or at least punished us in some way. But he did not. Was he a former cool cat himself? It made me wonder. After his departure, we few remaining flunkies openly and loudly discussed what had just transpired. How did he know about the party? Did we have a narc in our midst that reported to him about our every indiscretion and act of nonconformity? Why was an old man up so late, anyway? However, perhaps in the dean's eyes we were the new norm, the new reality, for the time period. This is what a silent minority of pharmacy students did in their down time, and he couldn't change that. I believe he did the best he could with the *bad boys* and *girls* he had to educate and graduate. That was his cross to bear; at least I appreciated it *and* him. He wasn't such a *nudge,* or *putz,* after all.

84

Tennis Club?

It sounded so inviting, so tempting, so clubbish and snobbish. Did our college really have one? How come no one had told me about it earlier? Was it a real team? Did we have hidden tennis courts somewhere? We had real varsity teams, such as basketball and soccer. The men's basketball teams at the time were very good and had a large fan base, often winning consecutive league championships. But tennis? All those questions were answered on that dreary and rainy spring day at an ad hoc tennis meeting in the student union. I was a fourth-year student and had only played during the summer breaks but I decided to attend the meeting, if just to meet some players to hit with. I didn't play costly indoor tennis and was rusty, and no longer had the time or desire to search out players to play on a consistent basis. Like all sports, you either use it or lose it. I was a decent former high school player, though. I was ranked first in Section IV, Class B by my junior year. I only lost four times in high school and had won a few local tournaments. My old man had

been a college professor and tennis coach and taught me
the rudiments of the game. However, it was difficult trying
to play in pharmacy college. We had no team, nothing, as
far as I knew. Then, that meeting notice went up. D.M.,
a senior, decided to organize an official tennis team. He
got permission from the dean, who wholeheartedly and
surprisingly approved the effort. The meeting was quick. Five
guys showed up, discussed their win/loss high school records
and current physical fitness levels. None of us had played
all winter or, thus far, in the spring. But our enthusiasm ran
high and our tennis ladder was formalized. D.M. was the
captain and made me the number one singles player. He
would play in the number two slot. He ended up calling
a few local universities, junior and community colleges to
arrange matches. Most of the colleges thought he was joking
and declined to play us but a few agreed to add us to their
busy schedules. Our practices were a joke, consisting of
running a few laps around a city park and then trying to get
on the busy courts to play some games. They were pathetic
attempts to get in shape and match tough. In contrast, my
old high school practice sessions were much more rigorous
and demanding. We were five woebegone pharmacy pseudo
athletes with racquets, and that's about all. We played five
teams and lost five times. Not a single one of our players
won a match, including me. Our doubles teams also sucked
and played horribly. Nevertheless, it was fun driving to

different colleges to compete, but our level was just not up to snuff. We were out of shape and our timing was way off compared to the hard hitting and consistent players we faced. Even the niggling community colleges beat our socks off. Our car rides home were often quiet affairs with only the captain giving us dubious encouraging words. The short season was soon over, we disbanded and I never played for the pharmacy college again. D.M. had graduated and there was no team the following year; I didn't make an effort to organize one. I was too discouraged. Fast forward to today. After dental school and residency, my tennis mojo returned. I am currently a nationally ranked player in my age group, have won numerous local tournaments, have my own tennis court, and play "religiously" two to three times weekly, year 'round. However, it had been an interesting experiment and lark to play for my pharmacy college all those years ago. Although we never had an official team bus or uniforms, at least the dour and usually sourpuss dean cheered us on. I wondered why? I found out why later, when I was applying to dental schools. Evidently there was more to him than met the eye, much more.

85

Emmanuelle

I dislike soft porn movies. If I was going to view some bodies intermingling on screen, I wanted to see the real deal, not a bait and switch or a tease session. I hate R-rated flicks, too. Either show me penetrating parts and the money shot, or don't bother to get me hot and bothered. However, the fair sex usually has a much different and nuanced approach to all things sensual and sexual. I was, and probably still am, a "Neanderthal" male with all its connotations. What can I say? After thirty-plus years, at least hottie blondie still puts up with me, but doesn't complain in the bedroom, as far as I know. However, on that night back in college, she coerced me to humor her and view a brand new *chick flick* at a local theater. It was all rather hush, hush, you know, to build up the suspense and crowd. I was surprised that it was going to be shown at all because the powerful Catholic diocese in our college town had previously and quite successfully banned the "blasphemous" film *Life of Brian*, by the Monte Python

crew. Anyway, the new film was advertised as an R+ rated
French picture about the TITillating sexual escapades of
Emmanuelle, the female ingénue. The theater was packed
and I didn't notice any priests in attendance. But you never
knew. It was a mixed crowd with lots of couples. Was this
going to be some kind of a love-training photoplay for
we inconsiderate and hopelessly horny and hapless males?
Wait a minute, what did I pay for? Well, the movie stunk,
at least for me. There was lots of grinding and moaning
with camera angles that omitted the juicy pieces at the last
seconds. Full frontal nudity was absent and male genitalia
was not featured. Plenty of butt cracks, though. The exploits
and sexy innuendos by Emmanuelle were blasé and banal,
with a tired story line about the same old hackneyed clichés
of making love in all the wrong places, with all the wrong
men. Boring! I could have written a better screenplay; hell,
my girlfriend and I could have been more believable had
we starred in it! Oh, well. The best part of the evening was
exiting the show hall. The lights had gone on and, what
an eye opener. Hottie blondie and I saw many pharmacy
college student couples in attendance, as well as many
pharmacy professors with their "spouses." And, was that our
dean in the corner, cowering and beating a hasty retreat out
the side door? Perhaps? Anyhow, it made sense for US to be
at that showing. It was very familiar territory. I couldn't say
the same for the couples we knew, however. Most were the

"conservative," fugly, stuck-up, and snooty sort. The kind
that would have ridiculed that film in public, yet there they
were, hopefully having learned about what hottie blondie
and I practiced daily, sometimes twice daily! All the couples
we saw sheepishly returned our glances, then quickly turned
away, in shame I presumed. The film portrayed nothing
new and was rather soporific for me; nevertheless, my
girlfriend enjoyed it. But sometimes even a "Neanderthal"
had to put down his club, stop pulling his woman's hair,
sit through two hours of never-ending foreplay fantasy, and
come out smiling. Wow. We didn't have sex later that night,
I was too distraught, and tired.

86

The Wine Shop

Fourth year was over! Not only was I a pharmacy intern working in my future father-in-law's drugstore, I was seeing quite a lot of his daughter, as well. Quite A LOT! That summer after my fourth year was a magical three months for me. I was living in a tiny but fully kitted out apartment, for free, above The Wine Shop, a wine and liquor store that my future in-laws owned in a nearby tourist village. I commuted to work in my trusty 1970 Plymouth Valiant to the next tourist town over, where the pharmacy was. My future wife was employed full time at The Wine Shop and we made every effort to meet up after work at that alcoholic emporium. She stayed late of course while I drove like a banshee to see her. And of course I sampled the goods around me, the liquors as well. We both became quite the connoisseurs of all proof libations that summer. I was off on weekends but she frequently had to do "family" time, away from me. I understood but was invited to many of those functions as well. Most

of those fantastic times were spent living it up at the
family's lakefront home while enjoying the cold beer, food,
swimming and boating. Initially, her family didn't take
us seriously as a couple and rightfully should not have.
After all, we were very young, had no money and were
just lowly pharmacy college students; although we did have
potential, as her Pop once remarked. We didn't press the
issue of legitimacy but continued to see each other as often
as possible. We stayed active by climbing scenic mountains
and often encountered black flies, deer flies, moose,
bears and tame deer on our treks. Eating at outstanding
restaurants was another treat. Who knew that such great
food could be delivered that far north? Attending the
annual Father's Day Frog Jumping Contest and winning
a local tennis tournament were also highlights that stood
out that summer. My stodgy folks even came to visit me a
few times and dismissively mentioned that the Dacks were
similar to the Catskills. Not really, but they had their local
pride, you know. Progressing as a couple and discussing
our futures, including the possibility of dentistry, seemed
natural and effortless. Of course on many occasions
those deep conversations were held with a couple of Slow
Comfortable Screws in our hands. We talked, we drank,
we slurred some more. I guess those repeated discussions
and our pervading passion for each other paid off. We
recently visited that same touristy village as a long-

married couple, without the kids and without many verbal exchanges. The Wine Shop is still there and long owned by another family, but it got us talking again about the past, the good times, the "profound" times, the "fun" times.

87

Fate or Tainted Luck?

I was working as a pharmacy intern in my future father-in-law's drugstore during the summer after my fourth year and still thinking about dental school. Yes or no? I needed some advice, some guidance, but from whom? In the coming fall I would be a senior at pharmacy college and had to get applications sent out, etc. Time was running out quickly. On an unusually slow day that summer, I was sent over to the local health center to hobnob with the physician, just for something to do and get some exposure to another medical field. I met the doctor and tried to socialize. He was seemingly bland but arrogant and "didn't have time for me," although there were no patients waiting. He dismissively suggested that maybe I should walk down the hall and meet "the dentist." So, I did just that. A kindly and gregarious man, he welcomed me with enthusiasm into his office. What a difference in medical demeanor! He was very busy with patients but asked if I wanted to observe. Fate, good fortune, neither? Whatever. I sat down in the assistant's chair and for the next few hours proceeded to avidly watch this guy drill, fill, extract, irradiate, mix, inject, etc. It was eye opening. I was actually excited, which was rare for me. I thanked him for the experience and literally ran back to the drugstore. I was thinking that I could do that kind of work. It looked easy. I believed that I could be even better than he, from what I had seen. My future father-in-law queried me about the physician but I went on and on about the dentist. It was beginning to become clear about what I should do in the fall: apply to dental school. And I did; however, as the school turned out to be, it wasn't as easy as I expected.

Take a powder paper!

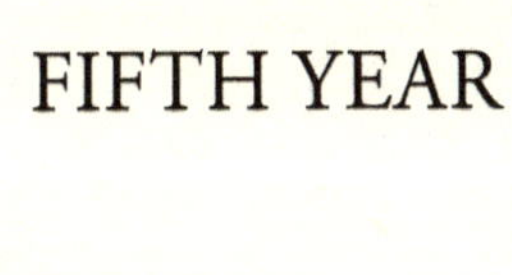

FIFTH YEAR

88

Senior Living

Well, this was finally it. Senior year, thank God! Still Apt.
3E, but a brand new roommate: the Foosball Wizard. And a
new *dental* attitude, but same old car and old lady. It was all
good, though. My previous roomie, of two-years duration,
had been itching to get his own pad, itching to get hitched
to his fiancée, and just itching to get on with life to get
ahead. Ahead of what, I don't know. Anyway, you know
the type. They have to go their own way because they just
know everything, are self-absorbed, and are firm in their
beliefs. So he and *his woman* got their own apartment and
bid me adieu before fifth year ensued that fall. We parted
as frenemies. Anyhow, during the late summer I scrambled
around to find a new roommate and, being rather well
known and connected, landed the guy I usually had sat
next to during the last few years in school. Duh. It was a no
brainer. I don't know why we hadn't cohabited earlier. He
brought his well-used bong and scales, I had the Smallbag
and dart board. A perfect union. He did bring some sparse

belongings, however, including a pillow, some sheets, his prize cooking utensil (a FryDaddy), a Rubik's Cube, a well-worn portable keyboard, and a malfunctioning squeezebox, which he stowed in his closet right next to his damn oboe! He also brought along that gorgeous pink-colored '65 Mustang of his, parking it in the spacious parking lot in front of our building, next to my drab, green Valiant. I owned the old TV, the furnishings, dishes, pots and pans, and mattress in the living room that doubled as a couch. But I also had "baggage"– my *hottie blondie* girlfriend. She was part of the living arrangements, although I was going to be absent many nights because of spending them at her place. It was all spelled out and fairly normal in those days. Many "pharmacy couples" dated, coupled and "played house" at their various living quarters and no one batted an eye. My new roommate was barren of girlfriend, but not for lack of trying. We all got along, though. It was cool. Plus, my girlfriend cleaned our place regularly, even the bathroom. Bonus. A new lease was signed with the same landlord who didn't care who lived there as long as we paid the rent on time. And another year began. Fifth year at that time was divided into trimesters. Everyone was together for the first semester, then half the class went on their externships and then vice versa. My roommate and I decided to alternate the last two trimesters but were together most evenings anyway. I chose the externship for the second trimester, he, the third. Half of the externship was spent in a retail drugstore, learning last minute ropes (most pharmacy students had already spent two summers doing internships in hospital pharmacies or retail drugstores), and the other half spent in a hospital setting, learning hospital pharmacy procedures. It was a stressful time trying to get your first choices of externship venues. Some students ended up loving their experiences; some hated it. I was in the former camp. My new roommate never did the two summer internships and was mostly clueless about pharmacy as a profession. He was going to pursue a post graduate degree after graduation, not take the pharmacy boards, and not become a pharmacist. But the externship was a necessary graduation requirement and we all did it. That fall of senior year was also consumed by me studying for the Dental Admission Test and applying to dental schools. Another headache, but one that I brought upon myself. I was determined to become a dentist and was vigorously doing all the chores necessary to get a dental seat somewhere, in any dental school. So in between suffering from incorrigible pharmacy courses like Therapeutics and Medicinal Chemistry, being taught by a no-nonsense faculty, my mind was also on dental school and my soon-to-be fiancée. Too much! My roommate was also consumed with a double life; finishing pharmacy college and applying to grad schools. It was all so damn hard at the time. I look back now and shudder

to think how we managed to keep our sanity. However,
we had our dart games, our mandatory after-dinner bong
hits, throwing-star competitions, pitch (card game) contests,
occasional parties and sex. Well, at least I had the latter
with my blonde beauty. We played darts daily, on a wooden
American dartboard, using wooden darts (we switched to
metal "English" darts just before graduating) with feather
flights. We didn't use a backboard. You can imagine what
the wall looked like next to the dartboard; full of puncture
marks and damn ugly. Lots of misses from endless playing
and using different distances kept the games interesting and
the wall pock-marked. Our accuracy prevailed one stuporous
night when we killed a mouse against the linoleum floor in
the kitchen. It only took six darts at close range. But, hey,
rodent eliminated! Chinese throwing stars got *thrown* into
the mix because of my fascination with Kung Fu. We both
got rather good at throwing them, either like a Frisbee, or
overhand into makeshift targets around the small apartment.
There were screwdriver-like indentations everywhere. I admit
we were somewhat malicious and hedonistic college grunts,
at times. We should have known better. Nevertheless,
whenever the landlord came by, he insisted on glad-handing
us and called us his "best tenants," in a thick Indian accent.
I guess other tenants were harder on their walls. However,
I can't remember if we got our security deposits back. And
yes, we still meandered to Roscoe's regularly to play foosball.

And I still played tennis sporadically with good local
high school players. My roommate played soccer on our
pharmacy college team, which sucked. To be honest, neither
of us excelled at our respective sports. But we managed to
keep in shape and tried hard at our athletic endeavors. My
girlfriend, roommate and I studied, toked and partied that
senior year together. Although she had two more years to
go, hottie blondie had had a taste of senior living with the
Smallman and the Foosball Wizard. I remember it all so
vividly and have a certain melancholy attached to those
memories. It was our senior year, dammit, yet my roomie
and I were just about to embark on long and grueling post
grad educations. We enjoyed being hip and popular seniors
but couldn't really capture those special moments for long;
there was just too much suffocating angst and uncertainties
about our futures to worry about. But that's life. And that's
what after-dinner bong hits were for.

89

Upperclassmen

As newbie pharmacy college freshmen, we idolized them, revered them, at least for a few years. They were the studs; we, only duds. Although only a few years our senior, upperclassmen exhibited all the hallmarks of distinction, privilege, and appeared larger than life. That's how low our self-esteem was back then. I'm talking about fellow men here, even though 50 percent of our college was composed of the opposite sex. Mostly menfolk hosted and attended the private mixers held all over town. Women, invited of course, came and mingled, but their numbers were usually scant. Anyway, those "seasoned" men were to be listened to, reckoned with, etc. I know I did my fair share of adulating them. B. and I sat around one Saturday watching WWF (before it became WWE) with the Hulkster, Andre the Giant, Bret Hart, Junk Yard Dog, etc., on the rabbit-eared boob tube, and began discussing our own senior status, between bouts on TV, and between bouts of darts and Pabst Blue Ribbon beer. I wondered

aloud if we also had fulfilled the natural order of things:
we freshmen worshiping the "elders" and then the new
frosh kowtowing to us, as the older mentors. Was it a
perpetual self-fulfilling prophesy? We reminisced about
how we had eagerly awaited attending those great parties,
be acknowledged by the older students as "regulars" and
get the blessing of belonging to something unique. Kind
of like a giant fraternity, or something. Those were relaxed,
fun times back then; no dorms, no RA's, no parental
supervision. Now I suppose most of those former kernels of
wisdom that were doled out to us by stoned and drunken
upperclassmen most assuredly proved useless in the end.
B. and I laughed. Were we seniors now also "required" to
nurture the young and the helpless? Misguiding them like
we were once misled? Of course! However, we never looked
at it in an imperious, patronizing sort of way and didn't
really remember any profound pronouncements coming
from our cake holes. If I had indeed pontificated something
important while simultaneously squeezing a bone, then
good for the bystanders. If not, screw them! They were
probably too wasted to recall much anyhow, like we used
to be. We matured very slowly over those five long years,
went to a billion parties and ended up dispensing our own
nuggets of hooey to the underlings. Were we held in awe
by underclassmen at those soirees? Most likely. I just hope
B. and I didn't warp anyone or create any wannabes. Hey,

we turned out OK in the end, didn't we? And I mean the bitter end. Much needed bong hits cleared our heads of that Saturday's philosophical digressive discussion and B. ended up hitting a turkey. I bowed to the winner, in jest, and cracked open another PBR can.

90

Senior Rebuild

It wasn't good enough that we were in our fifth and final year as pharmacy students. We were almost finished, and could taste it, but had to endure one more indignity– the complete and utter dismantling and reconstruction of our "glorified high school." It had been pre-planned, of course. And, nobody asked or had bothered to entertain our opinions. It just had to be. And so it happened, starting during our senior year and on our dime. After all, most of our tuition costs that year helped pay for the upgrades, I'm sure. But the substantial college endowment that had been sequestered for years also played a part in it. What a sight, and it began so quickly. It was all tall fencing topped with barbed wire, mounds of dirt, and colorful hard hats scurrying around. Heavy equipment was strewn around in close quarters, growling, pushing and pulling the heaps of debris to and fro. Our old and venerable, ivy covered institution was literally being torn apart at the seams to make way for necessary new classrooms, laboratories, library, and a large parking lot. Not to mention the upgrades to the already existing rooms and labs. What were our college dean, board of trustees and advisors thinking? All this time we students assumed they were hopelessly out of touch with reality and were a bunch of retro-loving oldsters. Well, it was time for a long overdue change; time to get serious about pharmacy education. For all my condemnation of the project and progress at the time, I guess it was vital to keep up with the future. It greatly inconvenienced us and we never got the benefits of properly working lab equipment, of labeled chemical bottles with tops on them, of a cafeteria with edible food that was open for dinner, and a library that had computers instead of a card catalog. We graduated and the project was finished. Darn it, just in time to leave. Since then, my alma mater has continually expanded and grown into a real college, with dorms, a soccer field and even a track. I hope today's students appreciate the high level of education and athletics offered there, although the way things are going, pharmacy learning may someday take longer than the current six years. Yikes, that's another story!

91

Applying

My mind was made up by the fall of my senior year of pharmacy college. I was going to be a dentist. Well, at least it sounded good. Now, about the application process. It would be easy, or so I thought. Senior year (fifth-year in pharmacy college) was difficult, and here my thoughts were on dentistry. Our school had no post grad office or administrative officer to aid students in pursuits outside of pharmacy. Because no one could or would help me, I was directed to the library to help myself. The old and mean librarian (typical, although she wasn't an old maid) cackled loudly after I divulged my future plans to her and pointed with a gnarly index finger to a row of books on colleges. She walked away shaking her head and wringing her hands. Not a good sign. Hours were spent in that damn small library researching dental colleges, application procedures, dates, fees, etc. Although I figured out that I had enough time to apply, the Dental Admission Test (DAT) really concerned me. The next test would be in mid-October. It was now

283

mid-September; no problem. I drove my old, but trusty 1970
Plymouth Valiant (olive green color, what else) to a Barnes
and Noble bookstore, purchased a Barron's DAT review
book and cavalierly felt confident about life and my future.
It was one of those beautiful sunny fall days when things
looked like they would work out. I forgot, however, that
Murphy lurked just around the corner ready to lay down his
Law! It cost $35.00 to apply to five dental schools through
a dental clearing house service. Why apply to any more?
Five seemed about right (I found out later that most of my
dental classmates had applied to at least twenty or thirty
dental colleges under strict guidance by paid advisors). I was
like the Fool in the major arcana of the Tarot: confident
but careless. I picked schools that were in my geographically
preferred area, sent in my $35.00 check and began studying
in earnest for the DAT. Sure, I still had to get other stuff
together– letters of recommendation, transcripts, personal
letters, etc.-but the looming entrance test took precedence.
It was only two weeks away! Fifth-year pharmacy courses
such as Medicinal Chemistry and Medical Therapeutics were
tough going, but, I managed to study that Barron's review
book as much as possible. I was going to be a dentist. After
taking a few practice exams, it quickly dawned on me that I
was either woefully unprepared or just plain dumb. Maybe,
both. These practice tests were hard and I just wasn't scoring
high enough to get in anywhere. Despair set in rather

quickly. And, those damn pharmacy classes just kept getting tougher and tougher, even while the school was undergoing a makeover. It was senior year; give me a break, for God's sake! The DAT exam was set up in sections comprised of sciences, mathematics, three dimensional reckoning and reading comprehension. Similar to the SAT but harder. I just wasn't ready. I needed more time! I decided to skip the October exam and take it in April, at the application deadline. I read that most schools would still honor the April exam, although they preferred the previous October results. No one told me that in reality, the April results were basically for the following year, not the current one. Boy, was I naïve. I got all the application materials together, minus the DATs, and sent them out. I would take the DAT in April and be all set. What a moron. That's how I applied to dental school: on a whim and a prayer. If someone had told me at the beginning what my chances really were or how difficult it was to get a seat in dental college, I probably would not have bothered to apply. But, I did. I was going to be a dentist!

92

Dentist Wannabe

The application process was well underway. DATs (Dental Admission Test)? That's another story! I needed two letters of recommendation. I asked a close family friend back home (character witness, and boy was I a character, even back then) who just happened to be a college president. His daughter and I grew up together; as a child, I practically lived on his front porch in the summers. He really knew me. For the second letter, I figured I'd ask the dean/president of my locally well-known pharmacy college, where I was currently a senior. Why not have two big fish write letters for me? I needed all the help I could get! Even I knew that much. My undergrad college was small; everyone knew everyone, and their business! Of course, the dean knew me personally, or at least it seemed that way whenever we passed each other in the school's hallways. He was a very short, stout, gruff, unfunny and decent man. Very old school. I was granted an audience with him after scheduling an appointment with his brusque secretary. Well, she wasn't really mean, just overly

and needlessly professional. As I entered his immaculate
office, he peered up at me from behind his desk while
scanning my transcripts, and in a gravelly voice said, "So, you
want to be a dentist, do you?" How did he know? Only my
roommate and girlfriend knew, or so I thought. Someone had
narked, but I wasn't surprised. Anyway, he shook his head
gravely while reading those damn grades of mine. It wasn't
a good sign. I meekly sat down across from him and asked
if he could see his way clear and write a letter on my behalf.
Silence. He pondered that question, scratched his balding
pate and removed his Coke-bottle thick glasses. Very sternly,
he finally blurted out, "We'll say in the letter that you were
in the top ⅓ of your class! It should help get you in." I was so
happy. The president of my college was actually going to stick
his neck out and help the class joker. What a guy! But why
would he help me, an insignificant peon at the school? I was
well known, but not for any scholarly endeavors. Was my B
plus average really that good; good enough for dental school?
Well, I thanked him up and down as I vigorously shook his
hand and prepared to leave when he suddenly told me to sit
back down. He had a story to relate to me. What story? He
now seemed a bit angry and spaced out. Uh oh! He proceeded
to spin a woeful tale of also wanting to become a dentist.
Who knew? After graduating from pharmacy college he got
as far as the second year in a very prestigious Midwestern
dental college. At the beginning of his second year he received

a dreaded letter, which he showed me, that bluntly outlined his "ineptitude" in the laboratory portions of his studies. You know, the parts that involve eye-hand coordination and three dimensional visualizations. Apparently, he just couldn't cut it (pun intended)! The letter, signed by the president of the dental school, ended with his dismissal. It was official, alright. I just sat there squirming in my seat. Awkward. My president still seemed bitter after all these years. Silence, again. He finally spoke and implored me to do better than he had done, to show "those bastards" that a pharmacy college grad could "cut the mustard," as he put it. I guessed my acceptance would be sweet vindication for him. However, it would still be a tough road ahead for me, especially without any advisory guidance. His mood brightened somewhat as he reverently stowed away that "sacred" letter of failure and started to talk tennis to me. It turned out that he was a nationally ranked player in the over 75's category. Who knew? And, who knew that he was actually a dental school dropout? His secret was safe with me. After he was canned from dental school, he proceeded to obtain his Ph.D. in pharmacy, began teaching and finally became dean/president of my college. I eventually did write him (before email, texts or cellphones) upon my graduation as a dentist. He wrote back a one sentence reply– "You did it for all of us." I guess I did. A little belated payback to the dental gods? I still have his one sentence letter, safely tucked away, somewhere.

93

Restashing

Please, say it ain't so. But it was; and it happened. And it was unbelievably embarrassing. The Smallman and his small band of like-minded souls had depleted their *stashes* to such a degree that a replenishment run was desperately needed. But, and a big BUT here, you had to know whom to trust. We purposely never procured "stuff" from the same person twice for fear of getting narked on, eventually. Familiarity not only breeds contempt but possibly arrest. We had a pow-wow; whom should we entrust with our next purchases? We knew everyone, at least I did, and everyone knew me. But I was out; we were all tapped out. "People" came to me and I shook my head; sorry but this *Head* had nothing to sell. Students "in the know" were keenly aware of our dire predicament. Then, someone surreptitiously slipped me a note in the hallway between classes; I didn't see who did it but I wished I had. It could have been a setup. My bunch was always wary and a bit paranoid. After all, we all wanted to graduate. We weren't deadbeat addicts just looking for a fix or quick high. There was a subtle science to it, some gamesmanship, some cloak and dagger stuff. At least it seemed that way to us. The note gave an address and phone number but no name and no reason. Fair enough. Maybe it was a lead? It was. I called and arranged a meeting with a soft-spoken, youngish sounding man. He was a frosh pharmacy student and had planted the note in my hand before skulking away that day. I knew the town very well and where Hudson Avenue was. It was a rainy Saturday afternoon as I rang the doorbell and was ushered into an obviously recently cleaned up living room. It smelled too fresh, you know what I mean? Three freshmen pharmacy students just stood there, staring at me, mouths agape. They knew who I was. I didn't know them from nothing. Very reverently they gave me a seat, gave me a complimentary *smoke*, lit it for me and kept staring. It's not always that the infamous Smallman graced a greenhorn apartment with his presence. I spoke first, but one of the freshmen interjected and gave me such a good deal that I shut up and let him continue. He was the ringleader of his little group and was visibly honored and delighted to *deal* with the Smallman. I came, I sampled, I exchanged green for green, and I left. I told my buddies about it and they were amused. Word spread fast at our college that the Smallman had to get his "stuff" from an underclassman. I shrugged it off but those freshmen from Hudson Avenue received a lot of street cred because

of it. I never bought from that rookie again: "office policy."
But we remained friends. He took my place as a purveyor of
all things Small after I graduated. I heard things, you know.
I also heard that he was an anesthesiologist at a prestigious
hospital after graduating from pharmacy college and medical
school, and practiced in California. I didn't doubt it for a
second. He always had a good *head* on his shoulders.

94

Truss Me

I had hated electives, thus far. Nevertheless, I had to take one more my senior year. We had a choice between Drug Induced Diseases, Radioisotopes, and Surgical Appliances. I signed up for the latter one. And it turned out to be a wise decision. The very first day of this weekly course set the tone for that fifth-year trimester. Mr. M. was a middle-aged pharmacist from New Jersey, owner of a surgical supply specialty drugstore, and an alumnus of our college. His son, the former tennis team captain, had recently graduated from our school and was his partner in "Jersey." In walked Mr. M., carrying a shitload of canes, crutches, trusses, colostomy bags, specialty bras, and compression hosiery, all while pushing a wheelchair forward with his foot. He unceremoniously dumped his voluminous load of "appliances" onto a large table in front of the class and started laughing. We joined him. It was a ridiculously funny first impression but a lasting one. While some brave souls wallowed miserably in the other two electives, we laughed our way to learning useful things that were often neglected in our education, but were important for retail pharmacists to know about. Such as measuring someone for an abdominal truss to hold in a hernia. Also how colostomy bags and products work. And what kind of wheelchairs and other walking/riding aids were available and how to determine the correct ones for the right patients. There was much, much more, as well. Mr. M. joked his way through the course but we learned so much. I loved it; we all loved it. Meanwhile, Drug Induced Diseases was strangling students' brains with extremely difficult medical material that was often over everyone's head. Radioisotopes, which my roommate B. took, was a mathematical nightmare; determining radioactive half-lives with geometry type proofs and deriving "hypothetical" isotopes from those complicated equations. Both of those tough electives were taught by Ph.D.s with no qualms about failing a faltering student. Meanwhile, our "Jersey" jester kept us entertained and informed about real world pharmacy that we could actually apply. However, my future wife did not take Mr. M.'s class when she became a senior. She took Drug Induced Diseases instead, and was murdered by it, and she was no dummy. She passed it though, like a painful kidney stone. Today, I still remember how to measure for a cane, how to walk with one and what types of tips are available. My wife just remembers the asshole professor who made life a living hell for her, senior year. And B., who the fuck knows what he actually learned from that crazy radioactive elective?

95

My Other Homes

Looking back, many pharmacy couples lived together, at least to some degree. Nevertheless, most, if not all still kept their individual apartments. Enter hottie blondie at the end of my third year. We became serious, fast and furiously, but had to uncouple for the oncoming summer break. The ensuing fall found us in two separate living arrangements. But it was necessary due to common sense and perceived decorum. What if we broke up? Then what? And we didn't wish to unnecessarily upset our relatively conservative sets of parents either. Besides, they were still paying the majority of our bills. So, we ended up keeping clothing and belongings at each other's places and played the "apartment shuffle," as did most of my pharmacy friends. During my fourth year I was still domesticating with my previous years' roommate, although at a new place and address (3E). Gradually his steady girlfriend became a "live-in" girlfriend. She literally moved in overnight; I guess I should have seen it coming. She had recently quit her second year in pharmacy college,

294

transferred to a local "easy" business college, and starting making marriage preparations. Things were moving quickly in their bedroom. In mine, hottie blondie and I discussed anything and everything, and decided on me staying at her lodging more often in order to give our two lovebirds in 3E more privacy. We had empathy and also sympathy for them both! However, my girlfriend's new roommates that year did not exactly show me the welcome wagon. Oh, they had all heard of the Smallman and his tarnished and studly reputation. They were uptight, tightly wound and testy around me. They were from differing pharmacy class years and my girlfriend was the extra, the fourth roommate in an already established hieratic henhouse. Things had been sort of copacetic until the Cock "moved" in. Believe me, my girl and I kept a lid on things; studied quietly, came and went quietly and TRIED to have quiet coitus. The animosity only grew, however. It didn't help that the previous year I had briefly dated a close friend of theirs. They obviously felt awkward at inviting her over with me there most of the time. The three witches made it known that my girlfriend had to leave at the end of that tumultuous school year; I helped her move the hell out of that hornet's nest and into a huge, four-bedroom home in a good part of town. Now SHE could be the queen bee and, as a third-year student, have some clout about selecting whom she wanted to live with. After reviewing paper resumes, she selected two very cute freshmen chicks, my "sweet tarts," as I referred to them, and a stocky, slightly lazy, slovenly but functional transfer student. This time, however, I was part of the package, the "fifth" roommate. All three new gals had steady boyfriends from home and tolerated the testosterone presence in their new home just fine. They figured out the deal quickly and actually enjoyed my company whenever I was around. But instead of calling me the Smallman, they affectionately referred to me as the B.D.O.C. Somehow, they just knew. I had also gained a new roommate, B., for my senior year but still lived in 3E. He also got the memo that hottie blondie was a package deal with the apartment. Plus, she would clean our bathroom, mop the floors and take out the garbage. What a deal. Everyone in our close circle of housemates "got it" and we went on with our lives, without much drama. Stay overs and trysts were now commonplace and normal, at least for me. What a difference different people make. It only took five years to get it right!

96

Therapeutics: The Professor Shuffle

Clinical Pharm.D.s and Ph.D.s rotated in and out of our Therapeutics class, and in and out of academia, as well. Those mostly intelligent "doctors" were often hired out of industry positions to teach us about how drugs worked in complicated disease states and in medically compromised patients. And often the reverse happened: one or more profs would "disappear" and head back to Pfizer, so to speak, often in the middle of a trimester. It was virtually a revolving door of expertise. The remaining clinical pharmacists took turns lecturing about their respective fields and often gloated over their specialized fiefdoms of knowledge. Some were glaringly arrogant and seemed to be put out by this whole teaching crap. A few couldn't believe they were actually back at their old alma mater trying to stuff "obvious" stuff into our pea brains. The rest of the profs were good eggs, and probably empathized with we bad yolks. Therapeutics was a necessary and valuable

297

course and, despite the shuffling of professors, actually taught we ignorant *nudniks* a multitude of pharmaceutical parameters; even to me.

97

Mistaken Identity

It was approximately 3 a.m. Saturday morning at 3E. Hottie blondie and I were barely awake, basking in the afterglow of post coital ecstasy. We were quietly laughing, talking, and about ready to drift off to slumberland when we quite unexpectedly heard a boisterous cacophony outside my bedroom door. What the hell was going on out there, at this hour? My roommate B. had gone out earlier with P. to hit some bars and have a few laughs. However, they had gotten ripped even before exiting 3E that evening. My girlfriend and I assumed that B. had returned home and was either asleep in his bedroom, doing some leftover "radioisotopic" homework, or playing with his Rubik's Cube for the zillionth time. Wrong! It sounded like a fight out in the living room with yelling, swearing and furniture being shuffled around. Now I was worried. I bolted out of bed with only my black briefs on. Briefs are better than boxers. How can any man wear baggy shorts underneath pants? It's inhumane. It just doesn't feel right. I don't care what my son says. I swung open

my bedroom door, burst through the wall of bamboo reeds
and beads hung up on my door frame, and in the low light
caught a glimpse of B. sprawled out on the cold floor, with no
other foe in sight. He was kicking an imaginary combatant
with his legs, like a cat does sometimes. Babbling incoherently
and in a state of hysteria and confusion, how did he manage
to get back home, I wondered? I bet P. had dropped him off,
but perhaps not? Did he drive his Mustang home, in that
deranged condition? Did he walk home and leave his pink
auto somewhere downtown? I called for hottie blondie's
assistance. She wisely turned on the lights so we could get
a better bead on B. He finally acknowledged our presence
and calmed down. Was he suffering from "stonosis," his
own coined word from toking too much? Was he drunk and
disoriented; or both? Perhaps he was traumatized mentally
AND physically? Crap, we weren't doctors. We didn't see
any blood and he wasn't clutching a body part. That was a
good sign. He was always a reasonable, logical, level-headed,
intelligent man. His histrionic actions thus far were WAY out
of character for him. My girlfriend and I gently maneuvered
him onto the mattress we had in the living room, took off his
shit stompers, covered him with a spare sheet, fully clothed,
and attempted to tiptoe away. He imploringly looked up at
us, swept away the sheet, sat up, and started enunciating. The
tale of woe he wove for the next hour made our skins crawl.
Our sleepy eyelids flew open in those wee morning hours; we

were all eyes and ears as we pulled up two chairs to sit in and listen. This is the unbelievable story he snorted out: He and P., his and my *smart* former roommate, had been on a major league after-quarterly-exam bender that night, doing more than a casual pub crawl. Finally, their *buzzed* evening ended and it was time to hit the pillow. However, B. had to pee, so he stumbled into a darkened, deserted alleyway, between two buildings on Washington Avenue, to do his business. Wouldn't you know that two cops had been silently tailing him, watching him the whole time, and quickly swooped in and tackled him hard, as if they were playing football. He didn't even have a chance to zip up. WTF man? But instead of writing him an appearance ticket or admonishing him for public urination, they forcibly cuffed him, stuffed him into the back of their paddy wagon, and punched it, tires screeching. He looked out the porthole window of the unmarked, and speeding police van only to see P. slowly driving away from the scene in his beat up Oldsmobile, while giving B. a puzzled look. B. didn't know if he was being taken to the nearest police station or what? And were those blue-clad goons really cops? In his schlocked and agitated state, he told us that he couldn't think straight. The van abruptly stopped and he was roughly dragged to his feet and onto a brightly lit porch where an angry looking elderly black man was waiting. Holy cracker! One of the white officers asked the old timer if B. was the one that had tried to break into his home. The homeowner laughed and said they got the curly hair part right but not the skin color. The cops released B. immediately but then B. protested loudly. He told the coppers that he didn't know where he was. They couldn't just leave him there, kicked to the curb, or could they? The black gentleman took pity on that crumpled pharmacy student in front of his stoop and implored the cops to take him home. The fuzz relented and drove him slowly and gently back to 3E. But what if that scared homeowner had also been wasted, or colorblind, and mistakenly identified B. as the alleged perpetrator? What if B. had somehow been railroaded into the police pen lock-up that evening and into a bogus confession? He had been drunk, out of it and defenseless. I doubt that a driver's license and pharmacy college I.D. would have exonerated him. The cops never apologized to him, either. However, the fates turned in his favor, in the end. He was safely home as hottie blondie and I catered to him. We tucked him back in, still with his white socks on, doused the lights, and went back to bed ourselves. My girlfriend and I lost sleep that night, B. passed out on that worn out and stained mattress, and P. had gotten home safely. Was it an unusual travail of college life? I don't know. But if that unplanned misadventure was the most exciting thing that ever happened to B. and P., then I pity them. But knowing them both as I did way back then, I'm certain that their future lives have been rich, rewarding and full of adventure! I can only hope.

98

The AMC Spittoon

It was senior year, the dean of our college was not well
liked, and our school was undergoing a complete external
and internal makeover. We students were just not in the
mood for more messing around. We were almost done
with this "messterpiece" called pharmacy college and
had to endure one more insult in a mess of mud, barbed
wire, concrete, and noise. Most male students were fed up
and decided to take their frustrations out on someone, or
something. Enter the dean's bright, red-colored automobile.
He parked it every morning in the small spot still allotted
to him amid all the construction going on. It was right
next to the side entrance of the college, where most of the
students entered. His car ended up being an irresistible
target for all kinds of monkeyshines, such as spitting on
the windshield, "adjusting" the tire pressures, physically
assaulting it, hurling insults at it, pouring water and coffee
on it, etc. Short of really damaging it, all sorts of vengeance
was reeked upon that helpless vehicle. However, it doubled

as an easy target of derision. Not only was it the dean's mode of transportation, but the now defunct American Motor Corporation's Pacer was a hopelessly ridiculed car by both auto pundits and the public. It was ugly, oblong with huge windows, and a source of jokes in the media at the time. It just added fuel to our already burning fires of dissatisfaction. Because he was relatively respectful and nice to me, having written a letter of recommendation to dental schools for me, I was deferential and respectful of his "metal carriage." But I never sold out the perpetrators of his car's eggings either. He knew how students felt about him and just rolled with the punches. He kept his car parked in that forlorn spot all year, wiped it off daily, and persevered in the rebuilding of his and our alma mater. I believe that car and the dean's stubbornness were symbols of his toughness and resolve to achieve his mission, regardless of our childish antics towards his automobile. He won and we got a brand new college. Of course, we had graduated by then and never had a chance to thank him, or his car, in person.

99

Mock Boards

You may be correct in assuming that there is something unappealing about that title. And, yes, the mock board exams did make a mockery of we almost minted pharmacists. However, they were necessary to take. How else could the school prepare us, other than use realistic conditions and grading? We students would then get a taste of the actual "game" environment and hopefully shed our jitters before the real boards were offered by the state. We seniors had to become adequately acclimated before officially executing the "real thing," well, the THREE "real things." The pharmacy boards at the time were composed of three parts: a multiple choice science/pharmacy section, a multiple choice jurisprudence part, and the "wet lab," part lll. Our class was confident that old board exams would adequately prepare us for the two written parts. It was the third part, the often confounding compounding session, that could easily derail even a stellar student. We were warned throughout the year to periodically restudy and review all our previous pharmacy laboratory manuals, to constantly jog our foggy memory banks. To help aid us, the administration went so far as to arrange a few mock board compounding lab periods, closely simulating the work environment, time constraints and state grading system. Our college didn't want any of we *scrubs* to flail and fail when it really counted. We were told in no uncertain terms to expect the unexpected; that there would most likely be the possibility of "curve balls" tossed into the mock exams on purpose, just like the state usually did on the real one. Great, just great. Why was this whole thing such a game, anyway? I'm sure some old, cranky, and demented pharmacist at the state level was already wringing her hands in glee, in anticipation of watching we worms squirm and squiggle during the real board exam. What was wrong with those board examiners? Didn't they get enough bong hits when they were in pharmacy college? Did they get ANY? Apparently not. All those future thoughts of already being a pharmacist aside, though, my fellow jesters and I braced ourselves to first get *mocked*. The "mock" grades didn't count, but we still wanted to do well. I mean we came all this way, putting up with five years of study, deprivation and cheap rolling paper. I TOLD my *buds* to only use Zig Zag or Bambu' and not Joker. But no, nobody ever listened. Anyhow, the day was selected and our class was corralled into our familiar large pharmacy laboratory for the "mock" experience. Well, nothing unusual happened

and my buddies and I were shocked. We had to choose two
out of three products to calculate, correctly compound, and
label. They were straightforward to manufacture. Most the
of class finished on time with correct preparations handed
in. It was a very auspicious beginning and we got plaudits for
our efforts. Not bad, not too shabby, I must say. However,
a month later, the next and last mock exam was a horror
show. It was probably intentionally rigged to showcase our
mental ineptitude as true chemists, to show us up for the
"frauds" we most likely were. To put a scare in us. Even
some of the brighter bulbs in our class went dim during
that time. Suffice it to say that we were manhandled by the
pharmacy calculations and formulations to be formulated.
We were thrown curve balls, sliders, knucklers and cut fast
balls that were unhittable. The cocoa butter suppositories
were supposed to be free of gravelly roughness. Nobody
would want to shove sandpaper-coated mini torpedoes into
a somewhat tender excretory orifice; nobody. The capsules
we had to make were supposed to dissolve in the stomach,
not on the countertop due to the caustic chemicals used.
What was that pharmaceutical trick we were supposed to
know? Shit. I forgot it. And the powder papers could not
be folded properly because of the miscalculated bulk of
powder per each one. Fail, fail, fail. No matter which two
agents were selected for compounding, each one of the three
choices had a wicked trick up its sleeve. Most of the class

flunked miserably. We flunkies got the message, however. We had to take our revision seriously, read up on obscure and detailed chemical transactions, reactions, and study our copies of Remington's, the bible of pharmaceutical sciences, "religiously" and with purpose. We had to wake up, as pharmacists. Our confidence was shaken, not stirred, and our work was cut out for us, even though we had been sorely and unfairly tested. I applied myself the same way I had diligently and methodically studied for the Dental Admission Test. I was determined to be ready and able. Five years of hard work wasn't going to be wasted, was it? I thought not. I was hard-boiled to be a state licensed druggist! It's funny how far fatefully futuristic and wishful thinking can take you. Sometimes, nowhere. Sometimes, a state pharmacy certificate. And sometimes, into dental school?

100

The Dreaded DAT

No one likes standardized tests, well, at least I don't. One of my children does; he's an extraordinarily gifted mammal, however. Anyway, after studying on my own for months, I felt I was somewhat ready to take that dreaded dental entrance exam and get on with my life. I still wanted to be a dentist! I had sent my DAT application fee in earlier by snail mail (that's all we had back then, no online anything), and was set to take it at a large university in my town. I heard absolutely nothing from the five schools I had applied to and hoped that they indeed had received all my application materials. I guess I could have called to confirm things, but didn't. The day arrived and I was more than nervous. My girlfriend tried her best to calm me down. It was no use. I had gotten better on the practice tests but still needed to improve. And, the three-dimensional parts were mind numbing. It was bullfuck! I got into my trusty Plymouth Valiant, waved goodbye to my future wife, and drove slowly and deliberately to the testing site. People assumed I was an old lady driving that car; nobody honked or seemed pissed off while passing me. The running joke in the '80s was that many little old ladies drove Plymouth Valiants. With my methodical and slow driving habits, I fit right in. I really didn't know where I was going. No GPS, no specific driving directions, just a general idea where the university was. It was a Saturday. I managed to find the place and a parking spot and proceeded to enter the wrong building. Hey, they all looked the same to me. Because it was a Saturday, there were very few students milling around on campus. I had just five minutes to get to the test and there was no one to ask for directions. And, I had to pee. Finally, someone appeared exiting from a nearby dorm and I launched myself at that person. She recoiled at my boldness and told me where to go, but gave me accurate directions as well. I made it in time– to a bathroom– and then found a seat with no time to spare. I was sweating bullets as I looked around the large classroom. It was filled to capacity with about 200 would-be dental students, all serious looking and ready. Was I ready? I had my #2 pencils and they were sharpened! Before we started, there was the mandatory check of students with ID that matched the test, the obligatory pre-testing speeches by the proctors, and the announcement that the soap and knife portion had been discontinued. What? The *what* soap and *what* knife portion? All the other students exhaled sighs of relief. I exhaled, period. It turns out that all previous exams had a

special part where testees (I like that word) were handed a
bar of soap, a tooth figurine, a short lab knife, and instructed
to carve the soap as best as possible in the allotted time to
resemble the fake tooth model in front of them. And, no
do-overs. Instead of this manual dexterity test, there would
be an additional three-dimensional examination part on the
test. I was always good at carving things and gluing models
together. I might have carved quite a tooth out of that bar of
soap. Little did I know that during first year of dental school,
carving and modeling wax shapes were required ad nauseam.
I would get my chance and then some to whittle, chisel,
and mold to the nth degree. The exam commenced and, five
hours later, thankfully ended. It went okay. Some parts were
actually similar to the practice tests I had taken. Reading
comprehension was about pharmacy problems, which I hoped
I aced. I found out later in the foyer outside the classroom
that most, if not all of the students, had diligently and
professionally prepared for the exam by taking a Stanley
Kaplan prep course or equivalent. I had heard of him. But it
never occurred to me to take a prep course. Idiot! I received
the results about a week later. Overall, I scored an average
of five on a scale of one-to-nine. Just average, according to
the adjoining graph in the results packet. I got a nine as
expected on the reading comp. part. Maybe that score would
get me in, or at least get me noticed. All five dental schools
acknowledged receipt of said scores. Now, I waited.

101

The Coors Episode

Coors beer was not sold in the eastern U.S. back in the '80s, plain and simple. It was a popular brew out west and we easterners had heard of it. And you know the tale of the forbidden fruit. Things are always coveted and taste better if "they" are rare or hard to come by. Be it women, food or drink; you know what I mean. I had just left hottie blondie's apartment on a Sunday afternoon and was driving down Woodlawn Avenue with my driver's side window open, when I heard a booming voice yell out, "Hey Putz, how 'bout some free beer?" I screeched to a halt. Now, normally I wasn't much of a drinker but it was a hot day and I had heard all the right adjectives flung at me. I parked the old Valiant and looked up at a group of my pals, sitting on the second floor porch of their pad, popping some cold ones. I started to cross the street when a can came whizzing toward me. Of course I caught it in flight, cracked it, and thanked the thrower. But wait a minute, it was a can of Coors, the taboo beer. I had contraband in my hand! I hoped no cops

were around. I sat down with my peer group and starting
yakking. They all knew where I had recently been; a booty
call up the block, you know. As I sat there sipping that
golden beverage I remarked to myself that it really wasn't
that good. It was supposedly sensational, but it wasn't. My
former *smart* roommate P., from our Action Central days,
lived in that apartment with two others and plied me with
a few more cans. Everyone present was raving about how
fortunate we were to get a taste of this alcoholic nectar.
Each of my buds devoutly clasped his can as if it were
gold or something. It turned out that one of them, N.Z. I
believe, had bought a few six packs of the illegal suds from
a close buddy of his during a trip out west. Anyway, we sat
there drinking and sparked a doob, just to complete our
reverie on that beautiful and sunny Sunday. Today, I never
buy or drink Coors or Coors Light, for that matter. It's a
commonly sold lager now, even internationally I presume,
and I still dislike its flavor, or lack thereof. Was it all
hopped up hype and propaganda all those eons ago? I don't
know. Silver Bullet bullshit is what I say. Nevertheless, I
didn't want to be obviously rude back then and so I greatly
appreciated being honored with a banned beverage.

102

Med Chem: Bringing it Home

Up to now we had been bombarded by high-powered, intellectually stimulating and daunting courses preparing we neophytes for the world of pharmacy. It was necessary, you know. No one said it would be easy; we needed to be adequately prepared medical professionals on the front line, administering to patients daily. However, there was one more class hoop we had to jump through; the one that upperclassmen unanimously warned us about. The one that would bury the weak-minded. The one that could hold you back from graduation if you tanked in it. Medicinal Chemistry was known to blast the brains of many a student with its subtle, sublime but deadly professor, and advanced chemical information. I was nervous about this course, as was my senior roommate, B. Although pharmacy college thus far had painfully proved to me that chemistry was definitely not my forte, I had managed to understand and learn a thing or two along the journey. Med Chem had no lab, but it did have a demanding professor and ridiculously

complex exams. I swallowed hard on the first day of class
and steeled myself as best as I could. My posse and I still sat
in the back row, but for this class we all craned our heads
forward and made sure there was plenty of ink in our pens.
Dr. V. appeared jovial, well-mannered, soft spoken and
respectful of we senior dunces. This was rare because most
of the other profs looked down on us, and we felt it acutely.
He proceeded to describe the course. Medicinal Chemistry
dealt with observing the atomic manipulations of organic
compounds, thus altering their behavior as medicines.
Substituting a fluoride ion here and a hydroxyl group there
resulted in completely different drugs, with different side
effects and usages. It was a distillation of all the disparate
chemistry disciplines we had studied thus far and sought
to unify our thinking, chemically, that is. It was basically
applied chemistry. Initially I thought this course would kill
me, but instead it made sense to me. I actually understood
chemistry for the first time in my scholastic life. I thought
Dr. V. was an excellent professor, thorough and thoughtful.
Although his exams were on the rough side, I managed
an 89 as my final average. Not bad for my aversion to all
things molecular. My apartment mate B. also did very well
and ended up pursuing Med. Chem at the doctoral level.
Ironically, as a fellow *toker*, friend and scholastic agnostic,
B. forsook pharmacy for medicinal chemistry, became an
insanely successful scientist and continues to discover and

patent useful medicaments for humanity. B., the Foosball Wizard, was never "weird" at all, just an annoyingly gifted and brilliant human being. Who knew? And me? My gift for humanity was pun-filled cornball comedy, and probably still is. It's the gift that keeps on giving; sorry. I am also currently serving out a 30-plus year dental sentence inside a miserable coffee maker that's also called the human mouth. You know, the same old grind! Dr. V. is long retired. His elegance and mannerisms in teaching sophisticated chemistry always stuck with me. Maybe I had finally matured as a serious student, just in time for his class. But perhaps it was the man behind the podium that resonated with me. An unlikely lecturer had convincingly broken through my thick skull and I was truly grateful. Thanks Dr. V.

103

The Interview— What the F…?

I only told my parental units about dental school after I
received an interview invite from PU College of Dentistry
in late April of my senior year, just after I took the DAT
entrance exam. Why build up hopes when you don't
have to? I was frosted by the other four dental schools I
had applied to; no interviews, no nothing. Although, the
University of Buffalo said I would be considered for its class
the following year. *Would be considered* was not the same
as an interview and/or admission. Plus, I didn't want to
shuffle off to Buffalo and be so far away from my soon-to-
be fiancée. My parents had a dumbstruck reaction to my
deadpan delivered news. Dental school? All kinds of inane
questions just kept pouring out of that phone receiver.
That's why I hesitated to tell them in the first place. My
father stated the obvious when he asked, "How the hell did
you get in with such bad grades?" Well, I retorted that this
was just the interview, and my grades placed me in the top
third of my class— just barely. Mom and Dad were old-

fashioned, somber, and highly educated college professors
and they understood higher education. Maybe that's why
they were so confused over my news. Only "those" kids got
into medical and dental schools. How did I manage such
a coup? I wasn't special, a "brainiac," or connected. But,
apparently this college wanted me, for some reason. Pop
finally did say that he was willing to shell out big bucks if
I was *really* going to become a "Doctor." His consternation
quickly turned to elation about my new career choice. It
suddenly became important to him and for the family
bragging rights. That's right: a doctor in the house! I had
to remind everyone that this was the interview, I wasn't
admitted yet. However, it was good to hear enthusiastic
people around me for a change. Even my very reserved and
stoic mother was giddy with pride. My father took a day off
to drive me to the interview. He knew the town well from
past educational experiences there and knew right where
to go. The four hour trip was filled with small talk– no
mention of the pharmacy college courses I had received Cs
in, or my girlfriend, or other hot button subjects. I think
he had new respect for me. Maybe? He double-parked
next to the "dental" building, wished me well, and waited
in the car as I disappeared inside. The security guard in
the foyer took my name, gave me a temporary "official"
badge, and escorted me to the elevator banks (there were
four giant elevators) with directions to the interview room.

I distinctly remembered this friendly guard with a thick Hispanic accent; we would meet again, soon. Many white-coated students milled about in the lobby and in front of the elevators as if in an asylum. I wanted to be a part of this lunacy; I just *knew*. I entered the "interview room" and sat down in the on-deck circle amidst a panoply of smug-looking, sharply dressed interviewees. Some were already finished and kibitzing, some were cockily bantering out loud. Was this display nervous bravado or were these jerks potential future classmates? Alas, you already know the answer. My name was finally called and just as I went through to the actual interview room I clearly overheard someone in that waiting room mention that he took the Stanley Kaplan interview prep course. Stanley again? What interview prep course? Boy, did I suddenly feel unprepared. This was not going to go well, and it didn't. I was already edgy from the long drive, the long wait and the Stanley Kaplan comment. However, it was my turn to be grilled, and brother was I barbecued! I sat down in front of two very dour-looking professors; one, the biochemistry chairwoman and dean of admissions, and the other, a "beloved" and long-tenured biochemistry professor. Why biochemistry professors and not dental professors (actual dentists)? I don't know. Well, both of them let loose on me like two untethered pit bulls. One blatantly accused me of wasting their time with my "low" grades, the other accused me of taking a spot away from an actual bio major because I already had a professional career (pharmacy). One demanded to know why I had two college presidents write recommendation letters? Weren't "lowly" professors good enough for me? This barrage of insulting questions continued unabated with only shrugs, nods and grunts from me. Finally, after another low blow, I spoke up. Big mistake. I rebutted every previous insult with a defensive remark and backed up every retort with logical reasoning, or so I reckoned. Well, my reckoning only made them more incensed. We three had a free-wheeling shouting match going on before I calmed down and stepped off. The last question shot at me was to identify– if I could– a butterfly from an insect book on their desk. I had mentioned in my application that I was an amateur naturalist/entomologist. Now I had to prove it! I got lucky. The butterfly was a common male Monarch butterfly and I easily and correctly identified it, much to their chagrin. I was then testily and brusquely asked to vacate the premises at once. I knew where I was not wanted, but this school did send me an interview request, hadn't it? I was confused and dejected. I had failed and felt miserable. It was way too late for Stanley Kaplan to rescue me. But then, out of nowhere, the portly biochemistry chairwoman scuttled after me and beckoned me to her private lair. I was hot, sweaty and angry, but followed her, all the while being stared at by the other

hapless students-in-waiting. She closed the door and glared
at me. Was this going to be more punishment, piling on?
What did I ever do to her? She bluntly asked me how I took
notes, how I studied, why I really wanted to be a dentist?
In restrained, measured tones, I answered as best I could.
She seemed to like what she heard from me. After a few
minutes, she ushered me out, smiling that "knowing" grin
at me. I guess she liked my act after all. I don't know if any
other potential dental student got the Part II interview from
her. Was I that good, was I the only sap with the audacity
to fire back when fired upon, or were they desperate for my
father's moola? Maybe two out of three? This had been my
only dental school interview thus far. No one else seemed
to want me. I remained cautiously hopeful, regardless of the
tumultuous interview ministrations that had just transpired.
My father had been waiting patiently, still double-parked,
for approximately two hours. He remarked at my slovenly
appearance. I quietly told him that I had been beaten up,
both literally and figuratively. We left the dental town. No
questions were asked, no answers would have been given.
I was wiped out. I slept all the way home. Hopefully the
madhouse I had just left would come through because I was
insanely ready to be a dentist!

104

Out of Gas

It could have been only a metaphor but it actually happened. Hottie blondie and I were driving over from my place to hers, on Woodlawn Avenue, on an empty tank when my Plymouth Valiant suddenly shuddered to a halt, right across the street from the pharmacy college. How ignominious. It was around 4 p.m.; labs and lecture halls were still full of underclassmen. I had managed to pull the car to the curb knowing it had run out of fuel. My girlfriend and I climbed out and sat on the trunk, thinking about our next move. Slowly, faces started to appear in some of the windows in our college. Then, some waving and pointing occurred, then some perceived snickering, as well. How did students know that we had run dry? I guess we shouldn't have been sitting there looking so miserable. Being a somewhat well-known pharmacy couple didn't help either. College was almost over for the Smallman; a few short weeks to go, to be exact. Maybe my ride was trying to tell me something psychologically. Was I also running out of gas? But I had that whole dental thing to look forward to, if I got in somewhere. I would be graduating soon and taking the final board exams right afterwards. I was tired; perhaps I was running on fumes and didn't know it. I quickly walked to the Mobil gas station a few blocks up, bought a gallon of gas and the gas can, and walked back to the car, lost in deep reflection. My girlfriend intuitively realized my introspective mood and blurted out, "'Doctor' Putz, fill up the car and let's get going, I think I see the dean laughing at us." Well, that snapped me out my pity party and put a jump in me. I emptied the gallon, tossed the container in the trunk and we skedaddled. I never told her about my exact thoughts that day, but I think she knew.

105

The Waiting Game

I had already thrown out the DAT review book. And
I already had my first interview with a dental school.
Pharmacy college was winding down and I was eager
and ready for more interviews and possible admittance. I
waited, and waited some more. It was now getting close to
graduation and pharmacy board exams. It was now or never.
Then three rejection letters in two days had me depressed.
All three commented that they could not seriously consider
me because I had taken the DAT too late for entry that
year, and all available seats were taken. The fourth school
replied that it would consider me as an applicant for the
following year if I chose to reapply. I could either use my
current DAT scores or retake the exam. I wasn't promised
admission but strongly advised to reapply. I was now 0 for 4
with one school to go. Meanwhile, I had a verbal agreement
with Rite Aid Pharmacy to work for it in my home town.
My parents were very happy; local boy makes good and
comes home. Or, should I say "loco" boy! They didn't

bring up the subject of dentistry at all, as if it was a non starter. My girlfriend was saddened not only for me but for the prospect of her possibly moving to my hometown and living close to my parents. Plus what would she do when she graduated from pharmacy college? My town only had one pharmacy. May 15th, a Saturday, dawned early, and we slept in. By noon hottie blondie woke up and went to get the mail. She came back and looked unhappy while handing me a letter. Her downcast look said it all. She held a white paper in her hand and had obviously read it. I snatched it from her and then yelled a profanity out loud. The school that had granted me the lone interview had accepted me. I could have killed her for purposely teasing me. We made up rather quickly, and her smile returned. Well, not too quickly. Finally, it was time to be a dentist. I couldn't help rereading that fateful letter over and over again. The first call went to my father. There was silence on the other end, then weak congratulations. How did HE get in? This kind of thing only happened to those OTHER brainy or connected kids. At least my mom sounded glad, sort of. (They had both been excited by my interview but then realized my slim-to-none chances of actually getting in. So they played down my prospects as a dental student and were literally shocked at my acceptance.) Rite Aid got the brush-off next. Call upon call was made until I couldn't think of anyone else to contact. My roommate B. came by in the afternoon to announce that he was accepted the day before to a Ph.D. program in medicinal chemistry at a prestigious college down south. Two of the biggest partyers and eccentrics in the class were moving on up in life. Who would have figured that? Of course we three celebrated with some rare *Hawaiian* herb that afternoon. My girlfriend was happy but sad that I would be far away from her for at least two years, until she graduated. I could tell by the look on her face that all of a sudden, she was uncertain of the future. Maybe living in my hometown didn't sound like a bad idea after all. It was a heady time, with finals, graduation, board exams, and dental thoughts all jumbled together. And this was nothing. Little did I know that my stress levels would be going through the roof in the very near future. I was a nervous wreck, already!

106

Last Day of Classes

It was the last day of classes for our whole college. Finals were the following week, however, then graduation, and finally board exams for we seniors. But for now it was time to unwind. As Vincent Furnier (aka Alice Cooper) would sing, "No more pencils, no more books…" Anyway, no one was in the mood to host or attend a real party. Most students just wanted to relax before finals and maybe sip a bloody Mary or two. No big mixer or fraternity hullabaloo was necessary, just some intimate social intercourse with significant others, partners and friends would suffice. And to share some beers and bones of course! And perhaps a bong hit here and there, as needed. Hottie blondie and I were finished by noon and walked over to her place to begin the "unwinding" process. Her three roommates were absent and must have joined their respective underclass friends for some socializing. Meanwhile, my girlfriend cracked open some Moosehead Lagers while I popped the cork of some cheap-ass Cold Duck champagne. We were all alone, drinking the two beverages in turn, laughing and talking about our futures, namely mine. Would I really make it as a dentist? Holy shit! Our conversations started to get too profound and deep. Time to bring out the Smallbag to calm things down, and *lighten* things up. We were already hammered when I lit a few cubes in some specialized glassware. The mellow vapors were sweet and sensual. Wow. The Smallman could still deliver the goods. It didn't take us long to polish off the beers and champagne, either. The time read 4 p.m. Too early for bed, or maybe not… The apartment was ours for the evening it seemed. Then things started to go downhill in a hurry, damn it. The doorbell rang and I answered. Big mistake. My closest friends knew where to find me and almost knocked me down as they raced up the stairs and into the kitchen. Oh, they were all there: P. and B., D., P.M., J.S., N.Z., B.B., D.H., and M.P. And they all brought *refreshments* with them. That wasn't what I expected. I could barely see straight at that point. Hottie blondie was the lone female present but was used to that particular paradigm with my gang. She was *cool* and they knew it. My buds trusted her and vice versa. But who the fuck brought that bottle of lime daiquiri booze? I should have thrown that shit out upon seeing it on the kitchen table. There weren't enough chairs for that makeshift party at my girl's place, but no worries. We dragged furniture and bean bag

chairs over; my girl sat on my lap. All set to *partee*, part
II. More hooch and hemp were consumed amid lively and
philosophical discussions about the ending of our time
at PP College of Pharmacy. Finally, someone mixed that
damn lime daiquiri liquor with added vodka. I never should
have filled my cup with that noxious whup ass drink. I
was already *gone* that evening and that sweet and tangy
limey crap was the clincher. Fortunately, my buds left at
that moment to "terrorize" another unsuspecting senior pal
down the street. Goodbye! It was late now and I hit my
girlfriend's bed face down and couldn't move. She stripped
and joined me, as usual. I started feeling sick, nauseous,
with hot and cold flashes. I had never had a serious
hangover or been in a drunken stupor before; now was
as good a time as any to show my vulnerable side. Hottie
blondie handed me a towel and her wicker wastebasket,
leaned me over the bed and got ready. What a girl, what
a girl! Then the dry heaves started; they were awful. And
then the knocking commenced. Here I was incapacitated
and barfing, my nude girlfriend was hugging and consoling
me from behind, and B. had somehow snuck back into the
house, most likely through the open front door, and was
banging with all his might on her bedroom door. Good
thing it was locked. He wouldn't stop and wouldn't take no
for an answer. What a guy. What a thoroughly WASTED
guy! He said over and over again, "Putz, I know you're in

there; get out here like a man so we can party some more."
This went on for some time until hottie blondie finally
had enough and admonished him for being so rude to
the Smallman, especially since I was feeling ill. B. finally
got the hint and left. Fortunately, her bedroom door was
undamaged. Her roommates never came home that night
and nothing was broken. A great ending to a fucked up
party, if I may say so myself. Finals were to start on the
following Monday. We all recovered quickly, studied like
crazy and passed, some of us with flying colors. Thank
goodness for my girlfriend. She had stuck up for me in my
moment of distress and weakness and fought off a raging
party animal, all while in the buff. Well, from behind a
closed and locked door, that is. She was a champ. I still
thank her for that timely moment of rescue over thirty-five
years ago. And I have never had a lime daiquiri cordial
since. Amen to that.

107

Gratuitous Graduation

Finals were thankfully over. Now on to step two: graduation. That was going to be the pomp and circumstance part of our college damnation; well, at least the *pomp* part. The *circumstance* was spoiled by an unconscionably stern and canned lecture by the keynote speaker, the lieutenant governor of our state. On paper, the graduation program held promise, but it ended up a disappointing flop. After perfunctory and platitudinous remarks by the usual asswipes, such as the dean, the senior class president and class valeDICKtorian, the very popular, elegantly attired and well-spoken lieutenant governor blessed us with his "magnanimous presence" and stepped up to the *mike* for his oration. We assumed his address would be chock-full of wisdom, hopefulness, pharmacy anecdotes, or perhaps specific encouragement for we newly minted druggists. Instead, it was a goddamn generic and rehearsed campaign speech which had been spewed forth all over the state on his "election" tour. Did he realize where he was, in front of whom he was droning on to? This was a pharmacy college graduation, not some whistle stop rally on his behalf.

We were irate that day, folks. Very angry and put out. What began as a joyous pomp morphed into we graduates becoming victims of his circumstance! His Honor went on and on about why voting for him was paramount, using the same old bromide of "helping the middle class" and dictating other half-truths and tired canards that clever politicians dispense when "on the stump." His spiel ended, nobody clapped, and students and guests dispersed with parental units in tow to celebrate. By the way, he was elected and became a two-term governor and kept virtually none of his promises. Duh. Well, he did keep a few silent ones, like hiking state taxes, expanding Medicaid, and raising state college tuition costs. It didn't pay to be "middle class" with him in power, after all. Anyhow, after that graduation debacle, my immediate family headed to a fine French restaurant where my girlfriend had made reservations. Our entourage included my parents, younger sister, my future in-laws and sisters-in-law, my girlfriend, and myself. I was already feeling kind of under the weather mentally when I was bombarded by the usual litany of annoying probing questions about future plans that I could not answer. There were discussions of future nuptials? I had just graduated and had not yet sat for the boards, but the vibe at the dinner table included my marriage to hottie blondie. I started to feel worse and worse. I hardly ate a morsel of Gaulish haute cuisine. I think the culinary masterpiece was excellent but the dining experience was an ambivalent and distressing affair for me. I just wasn't into it and all the well-intentioned and well-wishing people surrounding me. Perhaps I was ungrateful. But I had those dang pharmacy boards to get ready for, dental school on my mind and a future fiancée to reckon with. Lots of stressful stuff on the noggin of a 22-year-old. However, I lived to write this book about those tales nonetheless.

108

Boards

The real McCoy was soon upon us. We were still in the post euphoric throes of graduation bliss, however. Now my class had to quickly buck up, change gears and re-stretch our cranial cortex for the upcoming three-day board extravaganza. That was it though, the pay-off pitch. Unless you failed, no more studying as a scut-monkey student, ever again! If you passed successfully, you would be granted a state license as a registered pharmacist and could officially begin practicing. A few of my no-goodniks, including my stalwart senior roommate B., had taken the mock boards in good faith but, however, did not register or pay for the real one. They elected to omit it. B. was on his way for a Ph.D.; no pharmacy license was required where he was going. As for my other chums, I wasn't sure what had occurred. Perhaps they had some lingering incomplete senior requirements left, or had secretly failed a course somewhere along the line. The rule was that a student could graduate but not participate in the board examination process until all scholastic requirements were adequately fulfilled. A few years prior, I remembered seeing more than a few seniors "auditing" some of our classes to "fulfill" those compulsory academics. Nevertheless, board tests were offered periodically so every "technically failed" pharmacy college bozo had ample opportunities to become licensed. With me, since I was already accepted and enrolled into a dental school, I debated whether a pharmacy license was warranted. I had, however, previously sent in the requisite fee. And if I failed out of dental school, I could at least hit up Rite Aid for a *drug* position. So, gripping my sharpened Number 2 pencils, I took the boards, all three parts, on three consecutive days. Parts l and ll were easy, as expected. Part lll blew. However, all my extra last minute studying, like a butt nut, payed huge dividends. Our college had also been correct; the mock board exams had benefited we students tremendously. The compounding session, though tricky in some sections, did not bamboozle me. I chose the lotion and an ointment for my two products. I didn't "crack" the emulsive lotion while pestling the slippery ingredients in a large mortar, and the stinky ointment really was supposed to resemble dark fecal matter when properly spatulated and jarred in a small container. The stern looking state examiners didn't bother me in the least and I scowled in their general directions whenever I looked up at the wall clock to check the time. I wrapped things up, still scowling on purpose as I dropped off the labeled and finished goods in the lab. I knew I had passed. But I kept right on scowling as I left, just to piss "them" off. I hung around outside the lab that I would never enter again. Slowly, my exiting group of slightly discombobulated but still professionally attired pals formed a loose circle. B. and a few others were absent. We remaining five-year diehards smiled, shook hands with each other and parted company. There was no fanfare, no group hugs, no kissing, no coddling, no tears, and no long goodbyes. We had been through a lot and it was just time to go. For some of us, there would be more schoolin', for others retail or hospital pharmacy. We had made it. We were finally pharmacists and could now handle drugs legally. Perhaps a trip to Roscoe's to celebrate? Maybe not. Suddenly we seemed too old and mature for that crap. How sad. It seemed like just yesterday we were in our farcical fantasy land, joking and toking; and tomorrow, we would be diving head first into the dismal world of adult reality. And today? It had sucked, too. How sad.

109

Doing the Right Thing

It was late June. I don't know how I graduated and passed everything, but I did. It was all a blur. My girlfriend was working at the local VA hospital as a pharmacy intern and I was back home working as a pharmacist in a small pharmacy in an adjacent town, just for the summer. My mind was squarely focused on dental school, and on one more thought. Then in July I did the right thing by surprising my girlfriend with a visit and made her my fiancée. For a nonchalant type of tough mountain girl, she melted a bit. Phone calls burst forth and friends were made to look at that rock on her finger. She was going to be a "doctor's" wife. None of this had been in our future plans when we first started dating and mating. None of it. We were going to be pharmacists and that's it. This dental thing was either going to be a curse or a blessing. But I had to take the chance. Everyone gets opportunities in life, and some actually act on them. This was my moment. *Carpe diem.* What's the worst that could happen? I could fail out, my father would lose the tuition money, and I would be a Rite Aid pharmacist. A bad loss, but not that bad. However, if I made it, maybe someday I could own a beachfront villa on some island in the Bahamas. That's how I thought back then. Would it be worth it? Well, I did make it through dental school (summa cum laude) and now own two beachfront vacation villas, one on an island in the Bahamas and one on the Baja peninsula, in Mexico. And my hottie blondie fiancée? We got spliced in the early '80s and she still looks smokin' hot! I think I did all the right things. Perhaps.

110

Pharmacy Musings

Thank you for indulging me in this brief, opinionated piece on pharmacy and pharmacy education. These are only my opinions, based on observations, gut instinct, human nature, and most likely ignorance. Please, allow me: My much beloved and departed father-in-law attended pharmacy college for four years; my wife, sister and I went for five years apiece; the current generation is graduating after six years, albeit with a Pharm.D. degree as opposed to my B.S. The State Boards of Pharmacy, the pharmacy colleges and other whiners tell the public that it takes longer to graduate because there is so much more to learn and remember, right? Are those really valid reasons? What the HELL are computers, high tech instruments, and pharmacy technicians for then? Unless you are deeply involved in pharmaceutical research or, are teaching at a pharmacy college, or are some highfalutin lackey trying to play "doctor" in a short-staffed hospital, then I seriously doubt that longer is better. Maybe wider, but not longer.

That's what my wife says, anyway. I don't think it should take six years to learn how to dispense cheap wine, Playgirl magazines and cigarettes, along with Vicodin, from a drive-thru window at midnight at a 24-hour chain drugstore. And when I have intentionally quizzed cowering young graduates behind the counter about interactions and side effects, the telltale drug inserts invariably come flying out and get read from. Or "things" are quickly looked up on the all-knowing computer. I think you all get my point. It seems as though the disconnect between retail reality and pharmacy education is growing. So what will the future bring? I heard my college is already experimenting in a *joint* venture including physicians, named Homegrown Pharmacies, serving the underserved in various *seedy* locations. Are they really growing and selling *grass* out the back AND front doors? Who knew? Is it legal? Will it last? Who knows? And should we have separate pharmacy degrees of different lengths; for those that want to venture into retail (health insurance coding) pharmacy and those that choose clinical/hospital pharmacy or Pfizer? I don't know. There is already a myriad of choices at my old alma mater as far as degree programs go. Perhaps another choice is due? However, I hope things don't proceed as seemingly preordained: even higher college costs and more years to become "educated" as a pharmacist. If the college program becomes similar to a medical degree but without the surgery, future income, clout and prestige, then what's the point? Four years of prepharmacy followed by four years of pharmaceutical sciences, followed by a residency? Are you fuckin' kidding me? So remember, next time you are picking up Ovaltine and OxyContin from the drive-thru, think about the education of the "highly" trained Pharm.D. standing there like a dolt. Could the ever increasing pharmacy education race really be a big waste of time and tuition or am I just wasted and wistful?

Thank you for allowing me this venom-tinged digression.

111

Disclaimer for Pharmacists

To any pharmacist who just happened to mistakenly read this book in the bathroom before using it as kindling: you know what I'm talking about. We all suffer a bit from that ongoing dreaded disease called Aggravation Saturation; it started with our first pharmacy job as an officially licensed professional and never let up.

I sincerely hope you will have, or have had, a long and satisfying career in pharmacy. Not me. Although I successfully fulfilled my internship and externship requirements and worked as a pharmacist for a few summers during dental school, I never succumbed to the arduous and "mind-numbing" retail careers of most of my fellow graduates. Interestingly, more than a few of my close pharmacy brethren, and former fellow *tokers,* pursued advanced scholastic degrees like myself, and left the *pill-counting* world behind.

Was all that pharmacy college "fun" worth it? I think so. I definitely would have done it all over again. Of course, I'm not currently a practicing pharmacist and hindsight is usually 20/20!

112

Disclaimer for Students

To any prospective pharmacy student having read this book as gospel and still wondering if a retail pharmacy career is feasible: if you have scientific aptitude, empathize with humanity, and are able to stand vertically for long stretches of time, you will most likely succeed. Of course with today's automatic Pharm.D. degree, possessing a high GPA, having "connections" and *chutzpah* can land you a career in hospital pharmacy or the lucrative drug industry, instead. And an additional pharmaceutical/science M.S. or Ph.D. can really propel your clinical pharmacy momentum away from the *chain* gang. But let's face it, most of you will end up stuck behind the "bench," at Rite Aid or a Consumer Value Store (CVS). What can I say?

Hurray! You succeeded in getting admitted to and finally graduating from pharmacy college. If working in a retail chain drugstore is your dream job, as an absurdly learned and over-trained medical professional, now comes a *dumbing-down* career of standing, capsule counting, bottle filling, labeling, counseling, etc., etc. Oh, and not to mention selling prophylactics and Percodan from the drive thru window, arguing with smart-ass pharmacy techs and stupid doctors, dealing with insane insurance coverages, staring at the "all-knowing" computer screen all day, fighting with belligerent customers, not getting any lunch/bathroom breaks, etc., etc. Still want to be a do-gooder and save humanity with suppositories and calamine lotion, with no discretionary money for your *extra* counseling efforts? Burned out yet?

I went to pharmacy college not really knowing what to expect. Nevertheless, most of the courses were fascinating, informative and life changing for me. I learned about diseases and how to cure/manage them. How cool is that? But there was something missing from my ego. I sincerely thought I could do more for humans. Was I naïve, altruistic or just a *putz*? I don't know. I successfully finished the five-year pharmacy program, graduated, passed the boards and started dental school in the fall.

Do I regret not being a pharmacist? Not on your Nellie! Am I thrilled at being a financially secure but abysmally aggravated dentist for over 30 years now? Not on your Nellie! Maybe it's just me. Perhaps I should have earned a Ph.D. and become a bona fide entomologist after pharmacy college. No pills, no dentures, NO STRESS! But possibly no money, either. Careers and fate are fickle things.

Usually you only have one shot to get it right. I've had
two. Maybe entomology will be number three?
You never know.

Good luck!

113

Last Words

A few caveats. Firstly, I was the Smallman, a consummate joker, *toker*, partyer, eccentric, and eclectic card. But I was no fool. I was basically a connoisseur and aficionado of the *herb*, NOT a hard core stoner or lush. Reputations are funny things. I heard the "back room" buzz about me, reveled in my *illicit* notoriety, but studied my courses methodically and diligently. Secondly, this book omits the seriousness of the pharmacy college community, pharmacy students in general, and pharmacy as a noble medical profession. And lastly, sure, my buddies and I had fun, but there was always that undercurrent of responsibility and desire to graduate as pharmacists or "quasi doctors." We studied hard, played hard but knew our limits. No one got "stupid." Was pharmacy college worth it as an investment of time and money? YES! The superior science education allowed me to get into dental school. And I did meet and marry a *hottie blondie* pharmacist. Would I have done it all over again? YES, but maybe I should have seriously considered entomology as a final career choice instead of dentistry. Much later in my dental career I would sometimes reflect on my decision to "escape" from pharmacy. Did I merely exchange brick-laying for block-laying? Surely dentistry has been more beneficial to my ego and wallet than pharmacy ever could have, but not for my piece of mind, whatever small piece remains. However, it's not too late. Entomology may still be an option. Never say never. Bugs Я Us?

Thanks for the read.

About the Author

Dr. I. Mayputz (not his real name) graduated with highest honors from high school, from pharmacy college and summa cum laude from dental school. After completing a master's degree in prosthodontics at a then prestigious institution, he embarked on his dental career in private practice. He once briefly toyed with the idea of earning a Ph.D. to become an actual entomologist, but ultimately decided on a dreadfully stressful albeit lucrative career, instead. In addition to being an elite master's athlete, author, naturalist and part-time naturist, he is also known as a caustic wit and provocateur. He wrote this book to entertain family, friends, and any curious sod willing to peek through the crazy *haze* at pharmacy college.

For more alleged levity, please read
Dental School: A Bizarre Comedy by Dr. I. Mayputz.
Mr. Nick Productions, LLC., ©2015

WHO DAT?
PP COLLEGE OF PHARMACY
HOC EST, AN STULTUS
PHARMACOPOLA
MCMLXXXII